AMBRETTA LANE
STORIES

VALERIE GILFORD COLLINS

GROWN GIRL INSPIRED

GROWN GIRL INSPIRED

ISBN 979-8-9987894-1-0

Ambretta Lane map design by Amir Hamja/Fiverr

Printed in the United States of America

Published by Grown Girl Inspired

<u>www.ambrettalane.com</u>

DEDICATION

For The Incredible Characters In My Life:

My Family, who are my faith and foundation—there
for me since the beginning of my life story;

My Son and My Husband, who add mega doses
of sugar and spice to my daily existence;

My Friends, who lovingly and masterfully
expand my heart and mind;

And For My Readers, who I hope will be inspired by my
stories to create whatever makes their spirits soar.

AMBRETTA LANE
CONDOMINIUM COMPLEX

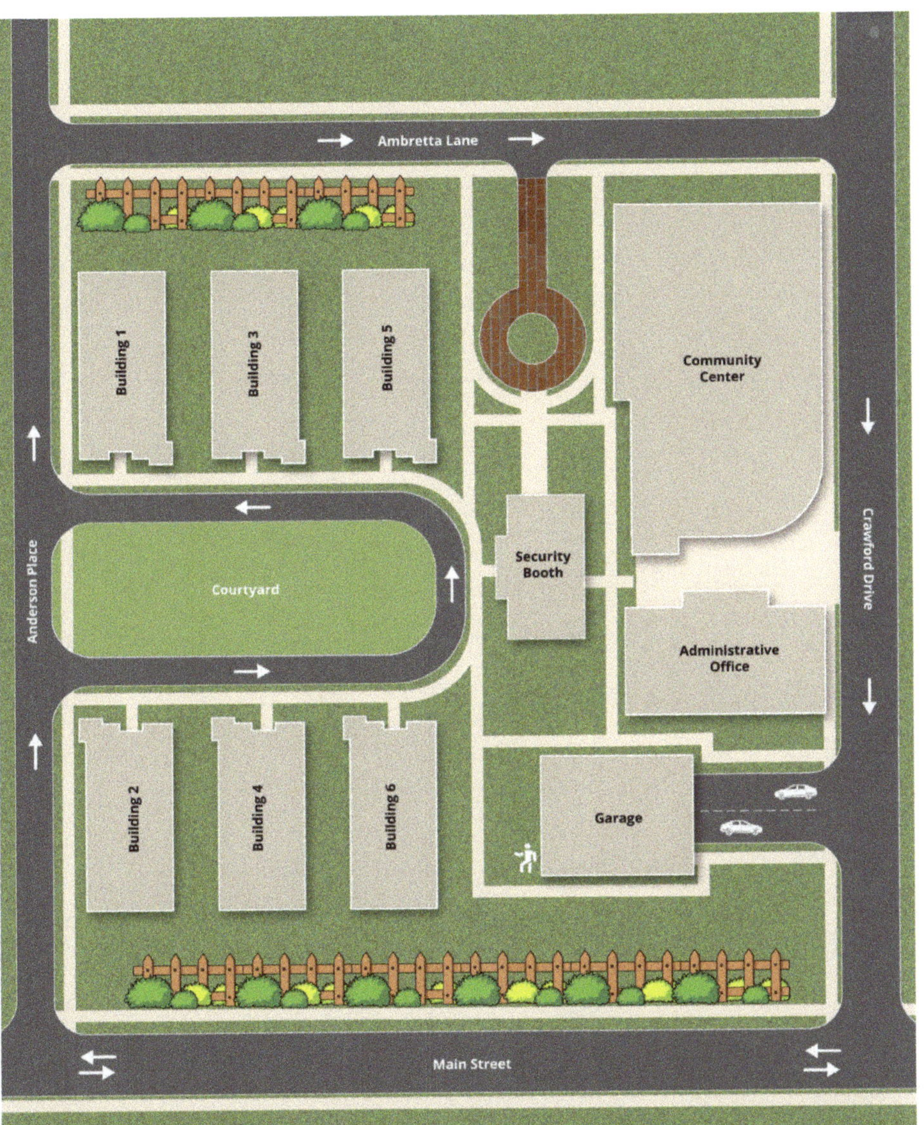

CONTENTS

THREE MINUTES 1

SUMMER MOOD 23

BITTERSWEET RETREAT 47

'TIS THE SEASON 72

I t had been a roller coaster of a March in New York, with no shortage of rain, a random snowstorm, and today, a crisp, sunny 52 degrees. It was half past nine and Erica was in the homestretch of her morning walk around Mabo Lake. The scenic 3-mile walking trail that featured beautiful wildflowers and fragrant pine trees was quickly devolving into the homey hustle bustle commerce that was Main Street. She could see the vibrant orange and green awning of Viv & Vera's Tea Shop coming into view. The myriad tea options were amazing and the decadent desserts were worth the extra mile Erica had to walk to burn off the excess calories whenever she indulged. Viv's mom, Vera, was one of the first people to open a business on Ambretta Lane twenty-five years ago, when she not only sold tea and pastries but also read tea leaves in the shop's back room. It wasn't something that

Viv was ever into, but she was fully aware that her mom still practiced it.

I'll pass on the reading, but an extra tall vanilla peppermint tea would hit the spot right about now, Erica thought as she whizzed past the store with the sweet herbal aroma of floral teas and sugary treats swirling around her nostrils.

Erica's walks refreshed her. She sometimes played the "behind closed doors" game in her mind when she passed by a seemingly so-much-in-love couple. *Nobody's perfect, she would think. Doesn't mean they aren't happy, but what's their story behind closed doors? Is she a control freak? Is he not ambitious enough?* Erica often wondered what people thought when they saw her and Allen together, cuddling at the movies or holding hands at the park. Did they come off as a happily-ever-after couple?

Main Street's eclectic mix of national chain stores, locally-owned businesses, and mom-and-pops welcomed the start of Spring with their collective door and window signage featuring "must-have merchandise" and "unbeatable sale prices." Erica had gone from dodging dog-walkers, bikers and joggers on the trail, to now weaving through baby strollers, food delivery scooters, and active senior citizens out for their daily quota of fresh air. Her regular route back home took her past the Dynasty Chinese Restaurant, Nell's Nails, Ambretta Lane Shoe Repair, and Walgreens, where she briefly stopped to catch her reflection in the store's window before walking in. She used her forearm to wipe a few beads of sweat from her face—her brown complexion was warm and blemish free. A blue fleece headband captured most of the moisture from her shoulder-length relaxed hair that was pulled up into a messy bun and was overdue for a touch-up.

One of these days, I'm gonna do the big chop and step into the beauty of my natural hair.

It was a promise she had made to herself for years and now at age 33, the promise remained broken. She had also promised herself that she wouldn't play it so safe when making life decisions, but she wasn't doing great on that one either.

Fortunately, Walgreens wasn't too crowded this time of morning with most folks in the community having already gone to work so she dashed down the Personal Care aisle and snatched a pregnancy test two-pack from the shelf. She hadn't even realized her period was late until she looked at her work calendar to plan her staycation this week. She hurried to self-checkout before she could be spotted by anyone she knew. The gossip game in this community was strong and she didn't need anything getting to Allen before she could talk to him. She made it out of the store and headed home to Ambretta Lane.

"Um um um. Looking fine as ever," Gerald said from the security booth that sat at the entrance of the complex. Erica was dressed in pale blue jogger pants that cuffed at the ankles, wore a matching drawstring hoodie, a blue and white geometric sports bra, and a pair of white Nikes. The outfit was by no means skintight, but it accentuated her slightly curvy 5'7" frame in all the right places.

She had to admit that regardless of how the compliment was delivered, it made her feel better about herself today. And today was a day that she needed all the positive energy she could muster. Today was the conversation she had to have.

"Gerald, I'm married," Erica said, smiling and raising her left hand to show him her simple rose gold wedding band for the umpteenth time.

"So am I," he said, moving his body to show off his once fit but now flabby physique. "But my wife doesn't appreciate me. Can you imagine?" he said with a straight face.

Gerald had worked at Ambretta for the four years that Erica and Allen lived there. Though he was head of security for the six buildings that made up the Ambretta Lane condo complex, it was doubtful that Gerald could chase anyone down if the situation called for it.

"Your wife is a lucky woman," Erica joked with the flirty older Black man.

"I know, that's what I keep tryna tell her!" he said.

"Have a good one." Erica waved goodbye and headed further into the condo development.

Flashing her ring finger was her signature move—confirming that she was spoken for, unavailable for a relationship. Funny enough, that was not always the case. The truth was that she and Allen had an understanding when they first got married. Not an open marriage, per se, but more of a flexible arrangement. It was Allen's idea all the way, but he was able to convince her that it was worth a try. Surely their love and commitment to each other could withstand an unexpected one-night stand or lunch hour dalliance, he had said.

Erica had known from a young age that she wanted to be married. She liked the idea of having a soulmate, a companion to travel through life with. She always thought that she wanted to be a mom too, especially since her own mom had made "keeping your man happy and raising a well-adjusted kid" look so easy. It wasn't until Erica's career started taking off that she realized there was always some level of sacrifice involved when choosing to start a family. Any maternal instincts she may have had about bringing a new life into the world were majorly dampened by the number of hours she had dedicated to achieving her dream job.

Her parents had been married for thirty-five years and they seemed mostly happy. She admired that. But there were rules and gender-specific roles in their relationship. Her dad worked and her mom took care of the home. Her dad earned the bacon and her mom cooked and served it. It was an outdated notion, but it worked for them. So when Allen proposed marriage to Erica five years ago in 2020, and then proposed the idea of the flexible marriage concept, she was open to it. Why not? They loved and respected each other, and she figured that he probably just wanted to feel a macho sense of freedom within the relationship. *How could freedom be a bad thing?* There was only one rule. They would draw the line when it came to having *serious* relationships outside of their marriage. Fun flirtations, a harmless hook-up, okay. Falling in love with someone else or having kids with them, absolutely forbidden.

Erica knew that Allen wasn't big on becoming a father because of his history with his own, but they never definitively said that they wouldn't have children, did they? They had just gotten used to creating their lives without kids and eventually seemed to prefer it that way. But then reality came calling in 2022 when Allen slipped up with a girl from the complex—Building One. Her name was Kim Shaw and she was four weeks pregnant by the time she told Allen about it. Kim had previously told Allen that she was on the pill or he assumed as much. Allen told Kim that he was sorry about the situation, but that he, under no circumstances, would leave his wife. He felt proud that he was honoring his unwritten marital contract with Erica by not having a child outside of their marriage. He had always said that he didn't really want to be a dad anyway because he didn't know for sure if he could be a good one. His own absentee father who abandoned the family was Allen's first and lasting impression of what fatherhood was and that became his guiding principle.

Erica was devastated when she found out about Kim's pregnancy. If Allen was going to start a family with anyone, it would be with her. And of course, she had heard about it from the neighborhood gossip, Mrs. Pruitt, who seemed to take pleasure in telling Erica every detail.

"Yes, dear, that girl was distraught," Mrs. Pruitt had said. "I heard she quietly got rid of the baby. What a shame—an innocent life. And Kim's a Catholic too. Her mom is devout. I'm surprised Mrs. Shaw let her do it unless she didn't know somehow. Anyway, a couple of weeks after that, she just packed up and moved out of Ambretta in the middle of the night. All because your man wouldn't leave you to be with her."

That was three years ago but Erica could easily recall the hurtful memory of Mrs. Pruitt spilling the beans that day and the heated conversation that followed between Erica and Allen that night.

"She's gone, okay. I'm sorry, Erica. I screwed up," Allen had said.

"Are you sure you screwed up? Are you sure this wasn't your way of getting back at me?" Erica challenged him. She didn't want to bring it up, but she knew that Allen was seconds away from rehashing the drama that had played out just a few months before.

"Oh, you mean you falling for your back-in-the-day boyfriend?"

"Yeah, I admit that I got caught up in my feelings for Noah, but we eventually ended it. Listen, this whole flex marriage thing was your idea and at least I was smart enough to use protection!" Erica didn't realize she was shouting.

"I told you. Kim told me she was on the pill. I believed her. Okay. It's over now, done."

Allen was wrong about one thing. Noah was more than just Erica's back-in-the day boyfriend. He was her ride or die guy during her formative young adult years and their connection was real. Noah Robinson was kind, smart, and giving. He was big on being active in the community, as his dad was a well-respected community leader who raised his kids to give of their time as well. Noah enjoyed helping people and it was one of the things that Erica loved about him. They met at a mutual friend's birthday party back in 2012 and within a few months had both lost, and found, themselves in each other. They dated exclusively from ages nineteen to twenty-two, and Noah had become the love of her life. He was her first real friend of the opposite sex and her first sexual experience. She was his Queen and he was her Boo, so Erica was crushed the day Noah told her that he was moving to another state.

"I don't wanna go, but I have to," he told her. "My mom can't afford to keep making the mortgage payments. My dad didn't leave her much, just enough insurance money to cover a few bills and his funeral." His dad had died from cirrhosis of the liver a few months earlier, but Erica had no idea it would result in Noah's family being uprooted.

"Where will you go?" She didn't really want to know because anywhere but there was already too far away.

"Arizona. Maricopa, it's near Phoenix. Aunt Nancy lives there and said she can put us up for as long as we need and help my mom get a job there."

"So that's the end of us?" Erica spoke through tears, tasting the salty liquid on her tongue. It was the fall of 2015 and it felt like it was the literal fall of their young and tender union.

"Of course not. There will never be an end to us, my Queen. We're soulmates, remember? Souls know no boundaries," Noah said, as he pulled her to him, kissing all the parts of her that he was sure he had just broken.

"Yeah, I remember," she said, forcing a smile and willing herself to believe in his words.

They stayed in touch regularly by phone during the first year after he moved away, with every conversation beginning with "Hi my Queen," "Hey Boo," and ending with "Love you, my Queen," and "Love you too, Boo." But neither of them was prepared for the amount of effort it took to make the long-distance thing work. They had only seen each other in person five times by the time the third year rolled around, and although the foundation of their relationship was still strong, the romantic spontaneity was tough to maintain. Erica remembered vividly the cold November day in 2018 when they became "just friends." Noah seemed to rush her off the phone a little. Not rude, just not their usual chat-filled conversation.

"You seem distracted. Everything okay?" Erica had said.

"Yeah."

"Okay. I was thinking about coming out there in a couple of…"

"I'm seeing someone," Noah blurted out so abruptly that he startled himself. "Sorry, I couldn't figure out how to tell you."

Erica said nothing. Noah didn't even hear breathing on the other end.

"You still there?" he asked. "Please say something."

"I…I just…I…don't know what you expect me to say." Erica finally took a breath.

"I mean, we're still friends, right?" he said. "I mean this long-distance thing has been real hard. I'm still here helping out my mom, and you're there getting your career going. I love you. I just don't know how to make a life with you from here."

Erica still had no words, but she knew Noah was right. They were both twenty-five years old and their lives were heading down different tracks. She had inadvertently put her social life on pause, having turned down quite a few dinner and happy hour invitations from male co-workers who had shown an interest in wanting to get to know her better. Of course, Noah was right. Their relationship had changed. It was ambiguous, at best.

"Okay," she said, almost whispering.

"Okay?" he repeated, trying to ascertain what she meant.

"Yeah. We're still friends." She realized that she just wanted him somewhere in her life. "Soulmates, right?"

"Yeah, soulmates," he said. There was an unintentional moment of silence between them to mourn the loss of the relationship that once was. "Okay. I gotta run. Bye, Erica. We'll talk soon."

Erica, he had said. No my Queen. No I love you. Just Erica. Just friends.

"Bye," she said, and with that, they both moved on with their lives. A year later Erica met Allen Jackson at a financial planning workshop where he was one of the panelists and she was immediately attracted to him. He was four years older than she was, had a secure job as a financial consultant, supported her career goals, and his model-like looks were a bonus. Allen was 6 feet 3 inches of melanin with broad shoulders, and ever so slight dimples that appeared when he smiled.

For the first time in a long time, Erica felt like she had it all: a thriving career, a serious relationship with Allen, and a renewed friendship with Noah. They had become close again over the years, despite the fact that Noah had anchored himself to Arizona with a steady girlfriend, and a position heading up a college prep leadership academy.

Erica's thoughts returned to Allen. She worried about how the impending results of the pregnancy test in her bag would impact her marriage. She wondered what their kids would be like. Would her daughter be numbers-smart like her dad? Would her son have Allen's dimples? What was she doing? She wasn't even sure she was pregnant. Her period had been late before, so it could be nothing. Erica counted on those ever-present questions in her mind to keep her at the ready for what life brought but waiting on the answers to every question before taking action was what often kept her stuck in place.

She walked from the security booth along a pristinely land-scaped path that led to Building Two, chuckling as she briefly looked back to see Gerald trying his best to win over another pretty female resident with his self-described invincible charm. Erica liked the diverse southern Westchester community, and other than the few indigenous gossipmongers and the new tech money types moving in, most of the neighbors were cool.

Erica reached her building, a 10-story high-rise with a façade that was identical to Ambretta Lane's five other condo apartment buildings. The six buildings which housed a total of 240 condo units were separated by a large courtyard with Buildings One, Three and Five on one side and the three even-numbered buildings on the other. The apartment complex was a haven for commuters who worked in New York City with easy access to a metro north train ride that landed them in midtown in thirty-five minutes.

Erica stretched out the warm muscles in her arms, legs, and calves, took a deep breath, slowly exhaled, and then entered the building lobby.

"Mornin' Wayne," she said to the cheerful lobby attendant.

"Hi Ms. Erica. Good run this mornin'?"

"Yep, just what I needed. Have a good day," she said as she walked toward the elevator. While waiting for it to come down from the top floor, she scanned through the four new text messages on her phone.

Promotion buzz. Def gonna be u. Njoy your vacay!

She responded to Linda's text: *Thx for the 411 & support, Linda. Appreciate u!*

Linda was one of the art designers that Erica supervised, and she was grateful that they had such a good working relationship. Erica had worked her way up from design assistant to senior creative director. She seemed to be a shoo-in for the VP title, but there were a couple of folks on her team who also had a shot at getting the promotion. The truth was, she wasn't a hundred percent sure she really wanted it. She used to call it her dream job, but now it felt like it was more about the satisfaction of reaching a career goal than it was about her actually wanting the higher position. She still loved what she did, and the salary bump would be incredible, but she wasn't quite sure why she wasn't more excited about it. In some ways, she felt like she was running in place.

She scrolled to the second text:

Hey chick, checking in—wanted to run something by you for our summer trip, call me later.

Her bestie, Charmaine. She and Erica had grown up in the same neighborhood, having met one another at age ten. Erica was an only child who enjoyed being a part of Charmaine's large extended family. And Charmaine, who was the youngest sibling of her three brothers, instantly formed a sisterly connection with Erica. So when Charmaine announced that after high school she would be moving to San Francisco to attend UC Berkeley and not coming back because "fuck snowstorms," Erica was heartbroken. Not that Erica blamed her, New York winters could be brutal. Charmaine had begged her to relocate to San Francisco after Erica graduated with her degree in graphic design from NYU in 2016, but Erica couldn't bring herself to do it. It was a decision that she regretted a little whenever she thought about it. Noah had just moved to Arizona and it would have been the perfect time for a change. But Erica was a creature of habit who thrived on stability and happened to love the unique vibe of living in the city that never slept.

Text number three caught her a little off guard:

Hey Queen. I've got big news. Call me.

Hearing him call her Queen still did a little something to her. She and Noah hadn't been in touch much since their brief fling ended three years ago. Their affair wasn't something that was planned. Allen was out of town for a couple of weeks for client meetings. Noah had been firmly anchored in Arizona and had come to New York for two weeks to train the person who was heading up a sister leadership academy program on the east coast. He called Erica as soon as he got to town and what started out as a catch-up over drinks swiftly turned into one romantic night and that turned into two weeks of reconnecting to a better version of who they once were together. But the reality was that Noah had a girlfriend and a life back home and once Allen found out about the affair, Erica's two-week high collapsed into a crushing low.

She scrolled down to the last new text:

Be home soon. Luv you A&F. A&F. Always & Forever. Erica wondered if Allen's "always & forever" came with conditions. She would find out soon enough.

The elevator was finally at the lobby. The door slid open and Mrs. Pruitt sauntered out like she owned the place.

"Oh hi, Erica. I rang your bell just a few minutes ago. I was looking for Allen. Is he around? I sure could use help placing some boxes and supplies in the storage room for the condo anniversary celebration."

"He would be happy to help, Mrs. Pruitt. I'll ask him to ring your bell tomorrow," Erica tried not to show her impatience with the pesky but regal 62-year-old woman. The Ambretta Lane 25th anniversary celebration wasn't even happening until the end of the year.

Truthfully, Erica knew that Allen didn't mind helping. He traveled a lot for work but when he was home, she appreciated how handy he was around the house. It stemmed from his up-bringing, coming from a family of all girls. His father had left when Allen was nine, his twin sisters were five and his younger sister was three. Allen never understood how his father could just walk away and it was the singular reason why having kids of his own wasn't essential for him. Erica was cool with that, until she wasn't. Until she realized that she would be thirty-five in a couple of years. Until she realized that she had achieved her career goals, so now what? Until she realized that her period was late. She had missed taking her birth control pills a couple of days in a row last month, having been distracted by heavy work deadlines and office chatter about the promotion. Now she might become a mom with someone who she wasn't sure would ever embrace being a dad.

"Oh dear, tomorrow. I thought he was expected back this afternoon," Mrs. Pruitt said.

How does this heffa know everything…never mind. Obviously Allen mentioned it to someone in the building who dutifully spread the word to her.

"I'll send him over first thing tomorrow, Mrs. Pruitt."

"Well, okay dear. I guess that'll have to be good enough. Enjoy your day!" she said.

Erica could hear music loudly pouring out of Reggie's apartment as she stepped off the elevator onto the fifth floor. It would normally be the kind of thing that would piss her off but she was partial to anything by Marvin Gaye, so hearing him sing the apparently unanswerable lyrics to "What's Going On?" didn't bother her in the least. She would have automatically classified Reggie as an annoying neighbor, but his playlist jibed with her musical taste, so it was all good.

There were four condo units on each of the ten floors, spread out into four wings. Erica and Allen shared their floor with Felicia, a flight attendant who was hardly ever home; Reggie, the self-proclaimed neighborhood DJ; and Mrs. Pruitt. Erica was certain that Reggie had something on Mrs. Pruitt because he seemed to get away with playing his loud music without reprimand or consequence. Mrs. Pruitt, who seemed like she had been through some things in her life, wasn't a typical busybody. She had a squad of folks who actively sought out gossip specifically to pass along to her. Some did it because she was in a position to reward them with VIP parking spaces or by looking the other way if they violated condo rules. But others did it so she wouldn't spill the dirt she already had on them. Mrs. Pruitt was the president of the condo board, which she apparently interpreted to mean that she was president of the entire community. She wielded her power like a jedi light saber slicing and dicing people's lives and reputations.

Erica's and Allen's 1200 square foot two-bedroom apartment boasted central air, hardwood floors, stainless steel appliances, and an ultra-modern decor. Erica walked in and dropped everything onto the entryway table as she ran to the bathroom. She had consumed a ton of water on her morning walk and her bladder was so full that she couldn't hold it long enough to open and unwrap the pregnancy test stick. It would be a while before she could pee again, so she showered, threw on some silky purple shorts with matching camisole and grabbed a protein bar to calm her growling stomach. It was almost 10:30am and she was exhausted so she crawled under the soft comforter that covered her wood sleigh bed. She wasn't physically tired from her morning walk, but mentally exhausted from running scenarios in her mind about what the rest of the day would bring. Erica woke up two hours later feeling refreshed but famished so she grabbed her phone and headed to the kitchen to find something to eat. Just as she finished the leftover beef and broccoli that she had ordered from Dynasty's the night before, she heard her phone vibrating on the granite countertop and tapped the speaker button.

"Change of plans," Charmaine announced. She always started conversations like she was already in the midst of one. Shortcuts. The benefit of a 23-year friendship.

"Let's do Tulum instead." Charmaine continued.

"Char, I thought you had your heart set on Cabo San Lucas? I already researched it and started planning an itinerary."

"I did, but then The Blog Chick said Tulum is the place to be this summer. It was one of the last cities built by The Mayans! Come on, be spontaneous with me."

"The Blog Chick. That name sucks. That blog sucks. And it's all over the place—travel, babies, sex, books, recipes, get rich quick, lose 50 lbs."

"We can't all be brand experts, Ms. Vice President of Creative and Brand Strategy."

"Yeah, right. Shut up."

"Erica, what are you having for dinner tonight? Personally, I'm popping a frozen burrito in the microwave, grabbing a jar of spicy salsa, some lime tortilla chips and ding! Dinner done in three minutes flat!"

"Three minutes, huh?" Erica said, almost whispering.

"Spill. What's the matter, girl?"

"I'm late. I think I might be pregnant. I was about to go pee on the stick and wait…three minutes."

"WHAT?!" Charmaine screamed through the phone so loudly that Erica turned the volume down.

"OMG, I should have put two and two together. It's you, of course it's you!"

"Calm down, you're hyperventilating. What are you talking about, Char?"

"I had a tea leaf reading from Ms. Vera a couple of weeks ago and she said that news of a pregnancy will change the lives of me or my loved one. And I know she wasn't talking about me because these tubes have been tied up like a pretzel knot for years! And you're my bestie—my 'loved one,' so it's gotta be you!"

"What?" Erica was confused.

"Yes, girl. Viv's mom does the readings remotely now. We did the whole thing over Zoom! It was awesome!"

"I'm nervous," Erica admitted.

"About being a mom? You'll be great! I call godmother!" Charmaine shouted.

"Of course you'll be godmother, Char. I'm nervous about Allen. I never told him about the birth control thing. I didn't think I could get pregnant from missing the pill just once or twice."

"Allen's a cool dude and all, but it's time for him to stop hemming and hawing about this dad thing. He already knocked up that girl Kim before when you guys were doing that crazy ass flex marriage thing and now you might be pregnant with his kid. He's a grown ass man. What's he gonna do, leave you because he doesn't think he can be a good dad? What kinda shit is that? Nobody knows if they're going to be a good parent or not until they become one."

"I know. I know. Everything you're saying makes perfect sense. "Char, someone's at my door." Erica said after hearing her doorbell chime. "I'll call you as soon as I take the test."

"Okay, mommy," Charmaine teased. Erica tapped the button

on her phone to end the call and made her way to the door, opening it to find Mrs. Pruitt standing there.

"Come on in," Erica said sarcastically, seeing that Mrs. Pruitt had already made her way into the apartment and taken a seat at the kitchen island. Erica closed the door and walked over to sit in a chair across from her intrusive neighbor.

"I'm sorry to have to tell you this, dear. But I just got confirmation about something I suspected, and word is starting to get around. I felt it was only right that you hear it from a friend."

"Word about what?" Erica was confused and wondered when exactly they had become "friends."

"The baby, dear" Mrs. Pruitt said matter-of-factly. Erica couldn't believe what she was hearing. Could Mrs. Pruitt have been listening at her door when she was talking to Charmaine about the pregnancy test? No. That didn't make sense.

"Mrs. Pruitt, forgive me, but I'm not sure what you mean?"

"I'm talking about the baby that your husband is having. With Kim. Kim Shaw."

Erica was frozen in place and sat dazed as she captured bits and pieces of the inconceivable words and phrases that tumbled from Mrs. Pruitt's mouth.

Eight months pregnant. Kept the first one. Looks just like Allen. Beautiful family.

Erica didn't remember moving. She didn't recall asking Mrs. Pruitt to leave her apartment. She had collapsed onto the tiled kitchen floor and laid there until she heard Allen's key unlock the front door some time later.

"Honey, I'm home!" he announced, dropping his keys on the glass entryway table. Erica felt like she had been punched in the gut. The pain of what she had just heard from Mrs. Pruitt sat heavy in her stomach like a ten-pound weight. She managed to pull herself up from the floor and walked into the living room where Allen was standing at the bar pouring a glass of wine.

"Want one?" he asked, extending the half-filled wine glass out to Erica. The glass shattered as it hit the hardwood floor, its ruby red liquid splattering Allen's white button-down shirt.

"What the hell?! Why did you knock the...?" Allen noticed Erica's expression and demeanor for the first time, and he was visibly shaken.

"Is it true?" she asked. "You fucking lied when you said Kim had an abortion?"

"Erica, let me explain."

"What's there to explain? You LIED! You have a two-year old son with her and now she's having your second baby. And all those business trips were just you building a life and a home with your side piece. Or am I the side piece?"

"Don't say that? I love you, Erica," Allen said, taking a step toward her.

"Don't you dare touch me! Get out!

"Erica, I couldn't leave her. She's the mother of my children. That's what my father did and I hated that bastard. I couldn't leave my kids, but I.....I love you."

"Leave. Leave now before I do something neither of us will recover from." Erica was heartsick as she watched Allen throw some things into a duffel bag and silently mouth "I'm so sorry" as he walked out the door. She knew that he would be back eventually but right now she couldn't stand the sight of him and she doubted that her marriage would survive the weight of the humiliation and betrayal.

The two hours that followed were a blur of flurried activity. She had called Charmaine to tell her about Allen and her best friend begged her to make a fresh start this time by moving to San Francisco.

"Girl! I'm not gonna say that I always knew Allen was trash, but I did always know that he wasn't a good partner for you. Hopefully the mighty heavens will spare you from being pregnant with his kid. But either way, now is the time to bring your rigid ass out to SF. I know a lot of folks so we'll get you a new job and I'm dating a realtor who can help you find you a great place. Until then, you can live with me and together we'll figure out how to deal with the baby, if there is one."

"Shit, Char. That's a lotta change for somebody like me who doesn't thrive so much on change. I don't know if I'm ready."

"You're 33 years old. You're still way too young to be so set in your ways. What the hell are you waiting for to start taking some risks?"

"I know you're right. Not making any promises but I will think about it."

In the midst of everything, Erica had gotten unofficial word from Linda that the VP promotion was hers…if she wanted it. And Noah had called to deliver the good news that he had texted about earlier.

"Hey there beautiful Queen. What's shakin'?" Noah's smooth voice was intoxicating.

"I'm good," she said, knowing that she was as far from good as she could be in that moment. She usually looked forward to any communication from Noah, but in the past couple of hours, she found out that she had been cheated on, learned that she had earned a promotion to VP, straight-talked and strongarmed by her bestie to try and relocate her to the west coast and now here was Noah with more news that she wasn't emotionally ready to receive.

"My mom is getting remarried after all these years. Remember the guy I told you she's been dating for a while?"

"The one she met at that Civic Space Park concert last year?"

"Yep, him. He has three grown kids and a couple of grandkids who live in Sacramento, so that's where they're getting married and moving to. My mom told me to make sure I invited you. It's in September, hope you can make it. I'd love to see you."

"I'm excited for her but isn't that kinda fast. They haven't been dating that long."

"You know my mom. She lives in the moment and he really is a good guy."

"Well then, I wouldn't miss Mama Robinson's wedding for the world." *Of course I could be eight months pregnant by then,* Erica thought. And that's when she realized that she still hadn't taken the pregnancy test. She mustered up the emotional strength to pee on the stick, then laid it flat on the edge of the bathroom sink. She contemplated how her entire life could be different in exactly three minutes. If it was positive, she would be a single mom. How would she work and raise a child alone, even with the help of her super friend, Charmaine? Would she really have the guts to relocate to the other side of the country and start over? Or would it be simpler to stay put, accept the promotion and focus on work until it was time for her maternity leave? Will Allen want shared custody? If she wasn't pregnant, would she leave everything familiar behind and finally take a chance to do something different, to be someone different? Regardless of the test result, she knew that her marriage to Allen was over.

Three minutes…negative. She wasn't pregnant. Erica stared at the life-altering stick in her hand for a moment. Ms. Vera's tea leaf reading had hit the nail right on the head: news of a pregnancy had changed her life, except it wasn't her pregnancy. It was finding out about Kim's pregnancy that had exploded Erica's life into unrecognizable pieces. She fully released the breath she had been holding, the feeling in the pit of her stomach beginning to ease. She realized in that moment just how much freedom she had. A baby would have meant sacrifice, sleepless nights, and constantly second-guessing if she was being a good mom. And while she was looking forward to experiencing the maternal joy of that someday, today she just wanted to be free to make choices for only herself. The pregnancy test became a test of her commitment to herself and she decided that she was finally ready to take a risk.

Noah. Mama Robinson. Charmaine. As much as Erica believed that her life was in New York, it dawned on her that her deepest personal connections resided on the west coast. She picked up the phone and tapped the screen, waiting patiently for the person on the other end to answer.

"Fuck snowstorms," she said, and that was the best shortcut conversation that she and her bestie had ever had.

Summer was in full effect on the streets of Brooklyn's Fort Greene neighborhood as kids of all ages released pent-up end-of-school energy onto playgrounds, basketball courts, and sidewalks. It was the third of July and Nicole wanted to get on the road to avoid holiday weekend traffic.

She closed the trunk of her silver metallic Jeep Cherokee after placing the last bag in amongst the two overstuffed backpacks already there, watching as her teen daughter, Reyna, locked the door of their brownstone and skipped down its wide steps onto the sidewalk.

"Ready, Sweetpea?" Nicole asked as she opened the driver's side and slid behind the wheel.

"The real question is sei pronta?" Reyna teased.

"Sei pronta? Translation, please, Ms. Italian class honor student."

"I asked 'are you ready'?"

"To see my mom, no. I would've gone to visit your grandfather instead if he and Leslie weren't on a Caribbean cruise right now." Nicole's parents had divorced in 2002 when she was 15. She adored her dad, Louis Pruitt, who recently retired from his medical practice and was happily remarried, living in Windsor, Canada. But Nicole's relationship with her mom was complex and strained. Claudi Pruitt had maintained her former husband's last name since much of her financial life was tied to it, but she had not maintained her relationship with her daughter. During the past year, they had finally gotten to the point where they were cordial to each other, mostly for Reyna's sake. But there were no Mother's Day get togethers, lunches in the city, Thanksgiving or Christmas family gatherings. Nicole hadn't seen Claudi in years and neither she nor Reyna had ever visited her at Ambretta Lane, so Nicole was caught off guard by the sudden invitation by her mother to spend the weekend there.

"Mom, can I drive?" the eager teen asked.

"Yes. Next month when you get your learner's permit," she said.

"Mom, c'mon please. Dad used to let me do it," Reyna said, still standing at the open door of the passenger side.

"Get in, Reyna." Nicole's mood shift was noticeable. She didn't want to hear about or think about Cal. He had been gone for almost two years and she was still grieving. Cal was a loving and fun person to be around. They had been married for fifteen years before a fatal motorcycle accident stripped him from her life. Nicole Pruitt and Calvin Hayes met at college, graduated together in 2009 and got married in September of the same year. Reyna was born in August 2010 and Nicole felt whole and complete.

She had been estranged from her own mother for several years and that had opened up a heart-sized hole in her soul. Enjoying her beautiful home in Brooklyn with Cal and Reyna, and her rewarding work as an art therapist, was the closest that Nicole had come to shrinking that hole into nothingness.

"Sorry, mom," Reyna said, plopping into the car.

"No, I'm sorry. I didn't mean to snap at you."

"It's okay," Reyna said. She scrolled through some photos on her phone and then abruptly clicked away from them. Nicole knew that they were photos that Reyna's friends and classmates had posted of their trip to Italy. Reyna had taken an immersive Italian class this past year in school and a couple of overly-involved wealthy parents decided to arrange a week-long trip to Italy this summer for whomever could afford to and wanted to go.

"I know you wanted to be there with them. It's just that you've never traveled without me or your dad and Italy is so far away. And I don't know those parents that well and you're only 15."

"I'll be 16 next month. Do you know what people my age are doing, mom? They're traveling, driving, dating, starting businesses, enjoying life. But you're so afraid that something's gonna happen to me, because something bad happened to dad, that you won't let me do anything." Reyna put in her ear pods and plugged into her cell phone before Nicole could get a word out.

Realizing there was nothing she could do to make it up to Reyna and figuring that there wasn't going to be much of a conversation on the ride, Nicole turned on the Blog Chick podcast. The Blog Chick started as a blog created by a married stay-at-home mom with two kids. It eventually spawned a popular podcast of the same name, covering far-reaching topics such as postpartum depression, sex life after kids, celebrity mom interviews, career choices and political opinions. The "Releasing Regret" podcast episode began with a question: *Is there anything you can do about it now?*

Nicole's main regret was that she felt she didn't always have her mother's love and support so she had completely shut Claudi out of her life. Cal had always encouraged her to let go of the past and make amends with her mother. Going to visit her this weekend for the first time ever was Nicole's attempt to start dealing with that regret. She felt guilty about not letting Reyna go to Italy with her classmates, so she couldn't say no to her daughter about the two of them spending the weekend with Claudi. She wasn't willing to disappoint her only child for a second time this summer.

Nicole glanced out the car window as she sat in a little traffic on the Hutchinson River Parkway feeling the three Hs of a typical New York City summer: hot, hazy and humid. She wasn't big on summer. It was a break from routine and she thrived and leaned on routine. Even as a kid when most of her friends bounced into summer from the last day of school, Nicole went into a bit of a depression. She needed the predictability and structure of getting up at 6am, showering, getting dressed, eating breakfast and catching the 7:30 local bus to school each weekday. And then on the weekends, going for a walk and being inspired by nature, then coming home to draw or paint what she had seen. But when unstructured summer came barreling through with its long hot days and warm breezy nights, it unsettled her. Her mother had always referred to it as her summer mood.

"I'll leave you be," her mom would say, "I see you're in your summer mood."

Now on her way to visit her mom for a summer weekend, Nicole was uneasy and unsure of what the next couple of days would bring. She put the address into her GPS and set off for the 90-minute drive to Ambretta Lane to spend two days with a woman she barely knew. The 62-year-old woman who was a condo board president and community leader wasn't the same woman who raised her. That woman, that Claudi Pruitt, was a manipulative and controlling gossipmonger who stepped where she wasn't invited, walked where she had no business being, and spoke from on high like she was a moral authority on all things. Nicole's teen and young adult years were miserable because of it, so when Nicole went away to college, she never looked back. And now at age 38, Nicole felt like she still didn't really know her mother and she never understood what had actually created the emotional distance between them.

"She's still your mom," Cal would always say, "Life is too short to hold on to resentment this long."

"That's not fair," Nicole would say to him. "So she gets to do whatever the hell she wants and I have to suffer?"

"Well no. You don't have to suffer. You can acknowledge what she did. Accept her for who she is and make amends. Or don't accept her and move on."

That was the part of Cal's laid back, live-for-today, attitude that Nicole couldn't get with. Her anger and resentment towards her mom served a purpose.

She decided that she didn't feel like dealing with regrets right now, so she turned off the podcast and tuned the radio to her favorite R&B station. She glanced over at Reyna who looked regal with beautiful box braids hanging down her back and over her shoulders with just a few colorful beads accenting the afro-centric hairstyle. Her light brown skin had olive undertones and her large expressive eyes resembled those of her father's. People always said that Nicole and Reyna looked alike because of their slender builds and prominent cheekbones, but Nicole always saw Cal when she looked at Reyna. She saw his free-spirited energy and aptitude for quick forgiveness shine through their daughter. She and Cal had done well. Reyna was compassionate, intelligent and humble. Parenting this smart, beautiful young woman was one of the things Nicole was most proud of in her life. She knew how important and defining the mother-daughter bond was and Nicole made it her business to give it her all.

"This was my song back in the day—J. Lo!," she said to Reyna when "Jenny From The Block" began playing on the radio. Nicole turned it up and bounced in the driver's seat, briefly taking her right hand off the steering wheel to wave her arms and snap her fingers to the beat. She saw a look of embarrassment on Reyna's face before it unexpectedly transformed into a smile and then a chuckle. They both sang out loud and danced in their seats for the rest of the song.

It was 2:30pm by the time Nicole turned into the condo parking garage, finding a space on the third level. She and Reyna gathered their things from the trunk and walked towards the security booth to get a visitor's pass. Two uniformed security officers stood in the midst of conversation in front of the large *Welcome To Ambretta Lane Condominium Apartments* sign.

"Make sure you store those boxes for Ms. Claudi. Put them in the storage room with the other stuff for the anniversary cele- bration," the heavyset officer with a friendly face said.

"Isn't that not happening until the end of the year?" the younger newly-hired security officer asked. "And isn't she the one who knows everybody's business?"

"Yeah, but we don't question what Ms. Claudi does and how she operates, just get it done." Gerald turned his attention to Nicole and Reyna as the other officer walked off. "Hi ladies, how may I help you two lovelies?"

"We're here to visit my grandma Claudi," Reyna said. She was clearly thrilled to be there.

"Of course! She said she was expecting her daughter and granddaughter and that it's your first time visiting here. Where you all from?"

"Not far, just Brooklyn," Nicole answered.

"Well, welcome! Ms. Claudi is in Building Two." Gerald said.

"Thank you, sir," Nicole said.

"No sirs here, just call me, Gerald. And enjoy the weekend, the Independence Day Festival is gonna be a blast!"

Nicole rang the buzzer for her mother's apartment, waited for the Building Two front door to click open and walked through heavy glass double doors into the lobby. She handed the visitor's pass to the building lobby attendant, and Nicole's stomach began somersaulting as they waited for the elevator. Reyna on the other hand was beside herself with anticipation and eagerness to spend some time with her grandmother to get to know her better. They stepped onto the modernized elevator with its gleaming stainless steel button panels and closed-circuit camera, lifting them to the fifth floor. Upon exiting the elevator, they walked past the wing that housed the two apartments on the left side of the sprawling floor and headed toward the two apartments on the right side.

Claudi lived in apartment 5A and as they approached it, they could hear music pouring out of apartment 5B.

"Grandma!" Reyna said when Claudi opened the door. They smiled and hugged.

"Hi mom," Nicole said, a little less enthusiastically, still trying to unravel the ball of knots in her stomach.

"Hi Nicole," Claudi said warmly. "How was the drive up?"

"Not bad. Just glad we made it before all the weekend getaway traffic hit."

"Come on in. You can drop your things there for now," Claudi said, pointing to the large foyer area.

Reyna twisted her hips and waved her arms as she danced her way into Claudi's apartment. "Sounds like somebody's having a party! Who lives there, grandma?"

"Reggie. He's a music teacher and a DJ. He'll be playing music at the event tomorrow," Claudi said.

"Any complaints from other people on this floor about the loud music?" Nicole asked.

"He's a good guy. Helps me out a lot. I'll introduce you all later. And as for complaints, I'm the condo board president so the buck stops here," Claudi said matter-of-factly. With that she closed the door and gave them a quick tour of her spacious apartment. There were three bedrooms, two bathrooms, and an all-white kitchen with top-of-the-line stainless steel appliances. Natural light from the large living room windows flooded the apartment and highlighted the beautiful artwork and collectible figurines that accented the room. The long hallway that led to the back of the apartment where the bedrooms were located was decorated with framed photographs of Claudi at interesting places, schmoozing with influential and prominent people. More often than not, Claudi was the shortest person in most of the photos, standing just 5'6 with heels on and 5'4 without. But her slight frame and imposing presence stood tall against any perceived competition.

Nicole always saw her mom as someone who was critical and controlling but the world seemed to see Claudi Pruitt as confident, straight forward and analytical in how she approached life. Having earned a bachelor's degree in business administration, Claudi began her career at age 22, working as an executive assistant at Metropolitan Bank. She married Louis Pruitt when she was 23, gave birth to Nicole at age 24 and was promoted to administrative bank manager shortly after. Claudi quickly rose through the ranks, eventually becoming Chief Administrative Officer where she prepared financial reports and improved the overall effectiveness of employees. The last few years before her retirement, she was pulling in $220,000 annually and walked away with a substantial retirement package.

Nicole supposed her mom was a success in every way—except being a mother. After college and at Cal's suggestion, Nicole had reached out to her mom once or twice, but Claudi always seemed otherwise occupied or "it just wasn't a good time." It was Cal who stayed in touch with Claudi by sending her pics and videos of Reyna when she was young. He even took Reyna to see Claudi a few times whenever her grandmother was in proximity of Brooklyn. When Reyna was old enough, Cal was the one who encouraged her to establish her own relationship with her grandmother. Nicole was initially upset when she found out because she didn't want Reyna subjected to the same kind of judgment and criticism from Claudi that Nicole had experienced. But Cal's death had drained everything out of her, and Nicole no longer had the emotional strength to put up a fight.

Maybe time had mellowed her mom, she thought, because it was evident that Claudi seemed to have a genuine bond with Reyna. The two were sitting side by side on the supple leather sofa in the living room.

"So how was 11th grade, Reyna? Any favorite teachers or classes?" her grandmother asked.

"Yeah. It was pretty good. My Global Studies teacher was cool and this was my second year taking Italian."

Knowing where the conversation was headed, Nicole quickly excused herself and retreated to one of the spare bedrooms to unpack.

"l'italiano è una bella lingua," Claudi said fluently.

"Grandma! You speak Italian? That's so cool! And yep, Italian is a beautiful language!" Reyna was impressed.

"Yes, I took a few classes in college and I've been to Italy a couple of times."

"Oh," Reyna said, her face falling.

"What's the matter, dear?" Claudi asked.

"My mom is so afraid for me all the time," Nicole heard Reyna say. "She doesn't want me to go away to college. She's hoping I'll go to NYU. What was your relationship with my mom like when she was my age, grandma?"

"To be honest, not that great. It wasn't always that way though. I never thought I would have kids and I was so focused on my career that I didn't even realize I was pregnant. I was 24 years old when your mom was born and it threw me for a loop at first. I didn't know who this new person was—me as a mom. But then raising her, teaching her, and loving her brought so much joy into my life. I wanted to spare her from hurt and pain. I wanted her to succeed in life and that's when I went into overdrive and I guess became overbearing."

"I mean, mom did say that you criticized her a lot and tried to make decisions for her," Reyna said wistfully.

"Yeah. You know what? How would you like to see some pics of your mom when she was young?" Claudi asked as she reached for two red leather photo albums from the built-in bookcase. Reyna flipped through the pages commenting here and there at what she saw and then stopped at one page in particular.

"Is that you, grandma?"

"Sure is," Claudi said proudly. Her diamond-shaped face was framed by a side-parted ginger updo back then, less conservative than the tinted light brown bob she wore now.

"How old were you there?

"I had just turned 30. I was a real looker, huh?"

They both laughed out loud and then spent some time getting to know each other. By half past six they were all starving so Claudi ordered fish tacos, crispy coconut shrimp and Caesar salad from Freddie's Fish Fry restaurant. After enjoying their satisfying seafood dinner and some small talk, Claudi took Nicole and Reyna over to meet Reggie. The 35-year-old, who resembled a young Shaquille O'Neal, wore a white "Music is Life" baseball cap, a gray and white "Think Positive" t-shirt and light gray sweatpants. The layout of Reggie's apartment was similar to Claudi's, but with a décor that was more function than fancy with a plethora of digital music equipment, instruments, and vinyl records.

"Nicole, hey sis! Reyna, little sis! Nice to meet you both. Come on in," he said, greeting them like they were family. They sat in his living room for a few minutes, chit chatting about the weather, about Brooklyn, and about how Reggie liked living at Ambretta.

"I like it here. And I love Claudi. She's very special to me," Reggie said. His words landed as a gut punch to Nicole's stomach.

"Reyna, why don't you stay and help Reggie choose some music for tomorrow's festivities? Give your mom and I some time to catch up." Nicole looked a little uneasy because this guy was a stranger to her. But Claudi gave her a reassuring look and in that one moment, Nicole chose to trust her mother.

As soon as Nicole and Claudi left his apartment, Reggie put Reyna to work. "I have some other music in that closet. You wanna grab it for me?"

"Sure," Reyna said. "How did you get into music?

"From my mom. She loved all kinds of music—jazz, rhythm & blues, classical.

"Wow, that's so cool."

Reyna pulled a box marked "60's music" out of the closet that was wedged between a couple of other boxes and caused something to shift in the closet. It was a large oil painting of a forty-ish year-old Black woman wearing a sleeveless floral print dress, sitting in an Adirondack chair with her legs crossed at the ankle, her hair swept up into a bun.

"She's pretty. Who is she? Is this your mom?"

"No, it's not," Reggie said.

"Actually, it looks like…"

"Let's get back to the music," Reggie interrupted her and placed the portrait back in its spot behind the boxes.

Nicole sat at Claudi's kitchen table and couldn't stop hearing Reggie's words in her mind.

She's very special to me, he had said. What exactly does that mean? He's young enough to be her son, Nicole thought. He's someone that Claudi made feel special and all I was left feeling was abandoned.

"So mom, why am I here? What's the reason we needed to be here this weekend?"

Claudi sucked in a long breath and exhaled, finally ready to release the words she hadn't been able to say until now.

"For the first time in my life, I started going to therapy. I know how people see me—as arrogant and a gossip. And I know how you must see me, the aloof but controlling mom who didn't love you enough."

Nicole hadn't sufficiently braced herself to hear her mom say out loud exactly what Nicole had been feeling all these years. She had no words of her own in that moment so she just sat and listened to her mother's revelations.

"My therapist, Dr. Savoy, is beginning to help me see that it was my way of dealing with my insecurities about not being good enough in the eyes of my incredibly religious and extremely unforgiving parents. I realized that it was time to start breaking the generational trauma of trying to control the people you love instead of simply loving them. Dr. Savoy encouraged me to take this step, to talk to you, and to really listen to how you feel. It didn't feel right to do it over the phone, so I invited you here. But before we talk about anything else, I want to ask, how are you?

"I'm good, thanks," Nicole said.

"No, really. How are you? I know these past couple of years have been difficult for you. Calvin was always decent to me and he was a good dad to Reyna."

"Yes, Cal was a great husband and dad. Just like my father was an amazing dad to me, but that didn't stop you from walking away from both of us when I was 15. You just divorced him and left both of us."

"I didn't leave you, Nicole. You chose to stay with your father. And in retrospect, you made the right choice because he was the better parent," Claudi admitted.

"I loved you both, but you were constantly criticizing me, mom. About the way I dressed, the friends I chose, the career I wanted. You even criticized Cal for being too laid back, not ambitious enough. I needed your love and support. That's why I stayed with dad. His love was unconditional."

"Nicole, I didn't know how to give unconditional love because my parents never gave that to me. They judged me, made me feel small my whole life. And I am so sorry if that's how I made you feel. It was never my intention. And what you saw as critical, was the only way I knew how to prepare you for the challenges of the world. I wanted you to make better choices for your life than I had made for mine at that time."

"So marrying dad and having me weren't good choices?"

"You were a beautiful result of a choice I felt obligated to make when I agreed to marry your father. And although I loved him, I was never in love with him. And I wasn't happy being married. And I'm ready to tell you why."

Reyna raced through Claudi's unlocked apartment door

the verge of tears but didn't want to give her mom the satisfaction of seeing her break down.

Claudi came back carrying a portrait. It was an oil painting that was the same size and on the same type of linen canvas as the one that was at Reggie's house, except that this one was of a different woman. The smiling woman in this picture was sitting in the same auburn wood Adirondack chair and had one of her legs loosely crossed over the other. The canary yellow sun dress she wore, with one of its spaghetti straps hanging slightly off her right shoulder, made her glistening brown skin stand out.

Claudi handed Nicole the painting.

"Who is this?" Nicole asked.

Claudi spoke with tenderness in her voice. "This is Gina. Regina Hargrove. She's Reggie's mother. And she was the love of my life."

Nicole's jaw dropped and an audible gasp escaped through her mouth. Had she heard that right? Did her mom just say that she was in love with a woman?

"I know this may be difficult for you to understand. I was 39 when I met her, just a year older than you are now. Your dad and I had been married for 16 years at that point. Your dad was busy working during the week and playing golf with his buddies on his days off. You were 15 and busy with school, your artwork, and your friends. And I was bored, not in love with your dad, and not sure of who I was. Then I met Gina. She was sweet, single, and had a 12-year-old son who was the result of a one-night stand she had."

"Reggie," Nicole concluded.

"Yes, Reggie. Gina and I were immediately attracted to each

other. I had never been with a woman before, but Gina had. She and I began to spend a lot of time together and every summer, we would go to Oak Bluffs at Martha's Vineyard. She was a singer and jazz musician. Because she was on the road often, Reggie mostly lived with his aunt. Gina and I listened to jazz, read to each other, went on bike rides, and soaked up the sun at Inkwell Beach. She was smart, sexy and fearless. And when I was with her, I felt like I was all of those things. She was my summer mood. I liked who I was when I was with her."

Claudi paused for a moment to see if she could gauge Nicole's reaction. On a scale of one to ten, with one being "I'm outta here," and ten being "cool, let's go see the fireworks," it looked like her stunned daughter might be at a 4, so she kept going.

"We were at an island festival one day where an artist was painting portraits. So we each had one done and gave it to the other person as a gift."

"So that's the portrait of you that Reggie has?"

"Yes. He asked me if I wanted to keep it, but I thought it should stay with him. He always said that the portrait made him feel good knowing that his mom had been in a relationship with someone who truly loved her and made her happy. Gina passed away in 2012, thirteen years ago, from cervical cancer. Reggie had just turned 22 when she died. I promised her that I would always look after him, which I did. Reggie lived in a few different states after that, but when he decided to move to New York, I got him a place here near me. For me it was like life was giving me a second chance to get the mom thing right. And by that time, you and I had reached a point of no return. I'm so sorry I wasn't the best mom to you, Nicole." Claudi said.

"Wow, mom, this is a lot. I had no idea. So you were…in love with her?"

"I was. That's why I wasn't as available to you. Because my happiness and wholeness was being with her and I didn't know how to blend my two worlds so I knew I had to let one go. So I chose the one that made me joyful, the one that made me feel complete. And I didn't know how to tell you both the truth but I did know that you would be better off with your dad. That's why I decided to end the marriage. I had been with Gina for seven months and knew that she was my life partner, my soulmate."

"Did dad know back then? Does he know now?"

"He didn't know specifically, but he knew that he didn't have all of me. He knew there was something not quite right. He called me the night before he proposed to Leslie to ask what he could have done better in our marriage. That's when I told him the truth," Claudi said.

"Wow. I wish I had known all of this sooner. Not that I ever gave you a chance to explain your side of things. But I get it. It wasn't really about me. It was about you trying to come to terms with who you really were and what made you happy, while also trying to handle the 'being married and a mom' life." A silent understanding between them was developing. They were both a little teary-eyed but were grateful for the release. Then Nicole unexpectedly chuckled out loud.

"I had hoped that you wouldn't hate me, but I didn't think you would take it this well," Claudi teased.

"I just realized how ridiculous it is that I've been an art therapist for the past 17 years and never once did I take myself to a therapist," Nicole said, and then turning more serious, "I need it mom, some professional help. I realize that now. And Reyna probably does too. We're both still grieving in different ways and I need to own up to my part in what my relationship with you is like."

"Was like." Claudi corrected her with a smile.

"Speaking of Reyna, there's something you should know." Claudi pulled a large manila envelope from between two binders that sat on her bookshelf and handed it to Nicole. "I set up a trust fund for her. She'll be able to access it in a couple of years when she's 18. This is your copy of the paperwork."

"I don't know what to say. When did you do this?" Nicole asked.

"The day after Calvin died. It was the least I could do for her, for him, and for you."

"Mom, this is incredible. Thank you so much," Nicole said.

"When I decided to be with Gina, it was the first time in my life that I had made a choice that was best for me," Claudi said. "I've made another choice. I've decided to step down from being condo president at the end of the year. For a long time, the influence and power of this position sustained me. But when I think back, I misused that power and influence in a lot of ways. I didn't always like who I was. Gina always brought out the best in me and since she passed away, over the years it became harder and harder to see myself the way she saw me."

"So what will you do now?" Nicole asked.

"Keep going to therapy. Keep close with my daughter and granddaughter. I don't know, maybe I'll travel the world. There are still quite a few places I'd like to experience," Claudi said. "And what about you? What plans do you have for the future?"

"I don't know. But what I do know is that I want to honor Cal and honor myself by living fully present and being the best mom I can be to Reyna. She deserves that and you just taught me that I deserve to not let fear stop me from exploring life and having a few adventures," Nicole said, feeling fully committed to the idea.

After a literally and figuratively explosive July 4th, Sunday morning's quiet calm was welcome and Nicole and her mom were at peace. Though she knew that she still had a lot of emotional healing work to do, Nicole embraced July 4th as her personal independence day.

Reyna hugged her grandmother, squeezing her tightly as she and her mom prepared to head home.

"Arrivederci, granddaughter. Until we meet again."

"Bye mom, and thanks…for everything," Nicole said, snuggling into her mom's warm embrace.

"We'll talk soon. Drive safely."

Nicole and Reyna sat parked in the Jeep Cherokee in Ambretta's garage. They both let out a sigh, looked at each other, and laughed.

"Mom, I'm so happy we did this."

"Me too."

"And you know what? I think dad would be really proud of you."

"Me too," Nicole said, touched by her daughter's sentiment.

"What a weekend, huh, Sweetpea?" Nicole said, having filled Reyna in on the revealing conversation she had with Claudi.

"I know. It was awesome. Grandma is so cool! And mom, I just realized, pretty much all of the tea leaf readings have already come true. The G letter in yours was referring to Gina and she was also the hidden secret. And for me, my good news was this!" Reyna picked up the large manila envelope. "I can't believe grandma started a trust fund for me. Can I see what it says?"

"I guess so," Nicole said.

"Mom, there's another envelope in here with your name on it," Reyna said after looking inside and handing it to her mom. Nicole opened the smaller envelope to find a check for $5,000 and a note that read: "The mother-daughter bond is something to celebrate. Go share an adventure with your daughter. Love mom."

Nicole pulled out her phone to text Claudi.

Thank you, mom, for the money and the motivation. I'm excited for what's next!

"Mom, what was that in the other envelope?" Reyna asked.

"I have a question for you first, Sweetpea?"

"What?"

"Sei pronta?" Nicole said, hoping she pronounced it correctly.

"Am I ready? Ready for what?" Reyna was confused.

"To help me find my new summer mood…in Italy."

BITTERSWEET RETREAT

Eden Waymond and her eldest daughter, Allison, were amongst the parishioners from Ambretta Lane and other surrounding communities for the Shaye Springs Unity Church evening service on this final Friday in August. Churchgoers were unsure of how to dress for the cool fall temperatures that had set in way too early for the end of New York's summer season. Millie Cruz, owner of Sweet Stems flower shop, wore a brightly-colored floral swing dress. Melvin Davis, a local community activist, wore slacks and a simple shirt and tie, and local librarian, Barbara Greene, was dressed in a single-breasted blazer over a white oxford shirt and a pair of black jeans. On their way into church, Eden overheard a couple of people congratulating Melvin on running for Ambretta Lane condo board president. She had heard that there were quite a few candidates vying for the position ever since Claudi Pruitt announced that she would be stepping down at the end of the year.

Unity Church had been Eden's spiritual home for the past twenty-two years. She liked the fellowship, the message, and the pastor, Reverend Matthew Saunders, who was set to deliver tonight's sermon. The heterogeneous choir launched into a soulfully stirring rendition of "*He's Able*," in front of the church's fifty congregants in attendance that evening. The gospel song was a favorite of Eden's mom, Dorothy. Eden's parents, Dorothy and Levi, were retirees in their mid-70s. They had raised Eden with a mostly hands-off approach, allowing her to make mistakes, fall down without them rushing to pick her up, and teaching her to trust in her own competence in making decisions. They were both former educators who now live in and teach English at an international school in Thailand. It was something they had always planned to do in retirement and hadn't ever regretted.

If only everything came together that easily for me and Donovan, Eden thought.

"Thank you choir. Good evening, church," Rev said, and the congregation responded in kind. "For those who are able, I would like to ask everyone to stand for prayer. Let's pray together so that we can be encouraged."

Eden stood and bowed her head. She definitely needed to be encouraged, especially with the dilemma she was facing. This would be her last year teaching at Shaye Springs Middle School as she and her postal inspector husband, Donovan, would both be retiring at the end of June. Eden would be fifty-five by then and she had already completed her 25th year of teaching. Donovan had been with the postal service for thirty-eight years and was looking forward to putting it behind him. They had agreed to a retirement plan where he would do more youth mentoring in the community and she would do some private tutoring and traveling with friends. But after Eden's weeklong trip to Atlanta this summer to visit her besties, Luciana and Sara, she came back with a new plan that Donovan did not appreciate. He minced no words about his frustration, and it turned into an intense argument where they both said things they shouldn't have. They were at a standstill but Eden was a woman of faith and she was committed to her marriage. The thing was she didn't know how to keep the marriage intact without losing herself in the process.

Eden hadn't realized that she was sitting in the pew with her eyes closed, her mind drifting. It took Allison tapping her on the shoulder to bring her back to present surroundings. She sat back and consciously pushed her muddled thoughts down for the next thirty-five minutes so that she could absorb the Word.

"Lord Jesus, we want to thank you for the excellent service we had today. Let everything we do be in line with Your Word. Be with us as we leave this place and grant us peace in our hearts. In Jesus name, we believe and pray, Amen," Rev said, bringing the service to a close.

As parishioners exited the church, stopping to compliment Rev Saunders on the evening's sermon, a distinguished man in his late 70s approached Eden and Allison. He was wearing a crushed velvet purple jacket that looked like it was more appropriate for smoking cigars in a dimly lit den than it was for praying in a house of worship.

"Sister Eden, you look finer than wine," he said grasping her hands loosely in his. "Brother Donovan sure is a lucky man to have you for a wife. Didn't see him at service today."

"Thank you, Brother Wilson. Donovan had some things to take care of for the back-to-school event on Sunday. It's good to see you," Eden said, "Give my best to your family."

"I certainly shall," he said as he took a step over to Allison. "Sister Allison, mighty nice seeing you here today, young lady. Splittin' image of your mama," he remarked. Allison and her mom both stood tall at 5'8" with legs longer than their torsos and both had the same sepia heart-shaped faces except that Allison sported prescription full-rimmed tortoise shell glasses that sat atop her nose.

"And how are the other alphabets?" he continued.

"Everybody's good, Brother Wilson" Allison replied, a little annoyed. No one had referred to them as "the alphabets" in years. When they were younger, the Waymond siblings were known as the alphabet kids because their names and the order in which they were born were the first three letters of the alphabet: Allison. Bryce. Celeste. It was Donovan's idea to have all the kids' names in alphabetical order so that the family's names went from A to E: Allison, Bryce, Celeste, Donovan, Eden. Eden wasn't thrilled with it but went along since Donovan felt so strongly about it.

The Waymond kids were mostly raised in Ambretta, having moved there in 2000 when the condo complex was first built and everything was brand spanking new. They moved into a three-bedroom apartment in Building One of the six-building southern Westchester condominium complex. Eden and Donovan had the largest bedroom, the girls shared a room, and Bryce had his own room.

Donovan and Eden met thirty years ago on his last night in Ochos Rios, Jamaica, when he was there as part of his cousin's destination wedding, and Eden was on the island alone mending a broken heart after she and her immature college sweetheart, Ricky, had called it quits. Ricky was a fun person and a great hang out buddy, but when things turned serious after three years of dating, his immaturity showed up as unnecessary jealousy and lack of commitment. So meeting Donovan was a breath of fresh air for Eden. He was settled, secure, and was a provider in every sense of the word. When Donovan met Eden, his love for her was immediate and his protection of her, automatic.

Shaye Springs was home to 77,000 residents and Donovan had lived there his entire life before he met Eden. The city had begun redeveloping the area in the late 1990s, so when Ambretta Lane condos opened in 2000, Donovan convinced Eden that it would be a great place for them to raise their family. Eden was twenty-five when she married 35-year-old Donovan and since he was so much older than she was, she almost always deferred to him or let him take the lead on their biggest life decisions. They had been married for twenty-nine enjoyable albeit predictable years, but Eden was thirsting for a little unpredictability. She was an only child who was born in 1970, an "uptown girl," raised in a Harlem community that was far removed from the abundance of brunch venues that populate it now. Her father was a professor at Hunter College and her mom taught at Cornell University. It was practically predestined that Eden would follow in their educational career footsteps. After she graduated from college, Eden's parents gifted her a few thousand dollars and put the apartment lease in her name before they left the country to start their post-retirement lives in Thailand.

Eden and Allison arrived home from church a little after nine that evening to see that Celeste was already there in the kitchen tossing a large quinoa salad. Celeste was a vegetarian, happily single, and the youngest of the Waymond kids. She had moved from home and now shared an apartment with her former college roommate outside of Philadelphia, not far from where they attended Penn State University. Celeste missed seeing Allison every day, but they were as close as sisters could be so physical distance was the only separation they ever experienced.

Allison and Celeste were spending the weekend with their mom to help with the back-to-school event. Eden was managing the event this year on behalf of Shaye Springs Middle School, in charge of organizing the food and giveaways of backpacks and school supplies for kids and teens in the community. With her own kids having attended the Shaye Springs educational complex all the way through high school, Eden understood the importance of such an event and was happy to help.

She kicked off her black pumps, took off her jacket, and put her bag and keys down in the foyer before sitting down in one of the padded stools that were placed around the granite kitchen island.

"How was church?" Celeste asked, having not attended since she was in her teens. She considered herself more spiritual then religious and preferred the individualism of meditation over the fellowship of congregation.

"Can you believe Mr. Wilson still calls us the alphabets?" Allison said. She had already stripped down to the shorts and camisole t-shirt she had on under the blue midi dress that she had worn to church.

"Well, you can blame daddy for that. Mom, why didn't you stop him when he was naming us in succession?" Celeste said, twirling an errant golden-brown curl that had fallen from her otherwise neat pixie haircut.

"You know your father," said Eden, who had gotten up to wash and dry her hands at the kitchen sink. "That salad looks good."

"Dig in!" Celeste said, setting out a couple of colorful plates.

"That does look pretty good. I'll have a little too," Allison said, watching her mom scoop up the lemony seasoned mix of quinoa, chickpeas, cherry tomatoes, and cucumbers. "This little break away from my boys is kinda nice!"

Allison still lived in the Ambretta condo complex, but in Building Four on the other side of the courtyard with her husband, Jace, and their twin toddler boys. She and Jace liked the suburban feel and diverse make-up of the area and its proximity to New York City where Jace worked as a sales VP for a bottled water company and dabbled a little in residential real estate.

"That husband of yours is a sweetheart, Allie." Celeste said. "One of these days I'll find a man like that but I'm definitely not looking for a husband—too much damn work. Plus, I just need to be free to be me. Speaking of husbands, mom, where's dad?"

"On his way. He was at the community center getting some things ready for the event. He just texted to say that he's stopping by Viv and Vera's to pick up some snickerdoodles," Eden said. Celeste and Allison looked at each other in a telling way and then turned their suspicious gaze toward their mom.

"What?" Eden asked, sheepishly.

"Dad is so predictable," Allison said. "Every time the two of you have an argument, dad brings home snickerdoodles. Every single time."

Allison was absolutely right, Eden thought. Donovan knew how much she loved that decadent cinnamon sugar cookie and he always used that to soften her up.

But not this time. All the sugar in the world won't sweeten this situation.

"So what landed daddy in the doghouse this time?" Celeste asked.

"Sara and Luciana want me to come to Atlanta to help run the B&B," Eden said.

Allison put her fork down and sat at attention. "Seriously? What did you say?"

"I told them I had to think about it. But the thing is, I really don't have to think about it. I want to go."

"And dad?" Allison asked.

"And that's why dad is bringing home snickerdoodles," Celeste said laughing.

"I haven't been excited about something like this in a long time. The place is amazing." Eden's mind instantly jumped back to three weeks ago when she first saw her possible future.

"Chica! You look hot, mama!" Luciana had said when Eden stepped out of the Uber that had pulled up in front of a Victorian style bed and breakfast. She had just arrived in the peach state to spend the week with her two best friends.

"This B&B is what looks hot. The curb appeal is amazing," Eden said as she wheeled her luggage and shouldered her bag into the welcoming residence that Sara and Luciana had named Glitter Cottage. It was a three-story home built in the early 1900s that exuded charm and southern hospitality. Restored in the past few years, Glitter Cottage boasted modern amenities like high ceilings, hardwood floors, marble bathrooms and a private garden. It lived up to its name, sparkling with gold glitter wallpaper, bling rhinestone accessories, pastel corridors, and ornate mirrors reflecting light everywhere. Vivid signage throughout the property made the benefits of being there clear: *"Stay here and find your sparkle."*

"Eden! Hey girl, get over here," Sara said as Eden came through the door. The three of them hadn't seen each other in a long while since Sara and Luciana were a few years older than Eden and had already retired and relocated to Atlanta to open the bed and breakfast. Their indelible friendship was formed when the three women worked together at Shaye Springs Middle School where Sara and Luciana both taught algebra. The ladies were inseparable around the school building, eating lunch together, sharing teaching strategies, and talking about their personal dreams and plans for the future. It was during one of those share sessions four years ago that Luciana informed them that she had inherited an Atlanta property from her grandmother that would make a great bed and breakfast. She and Sara did their research, ran the numbers, and decided to go for it. They had invited Eden to join them in the venture, but she had another few years of teaching in New York before she could retire.

"You guys are rock stars. This place is truly incredible. Sara, I can't believe you're stepping away. I know you have to take care of your mom, but are you sure?" Eden asked.

"I'm bummed about it, but I'm sure," Sara said. She had been handling elder care for her mother who had suffered a stroke recently and the weight and responsibility of it all had stretched her thin, physically, emotionally and financially. She eventually made the tough decision to sell her half of the B&B and Eden was the first person she and Luciana thought of to buy Sara out.

Eden was so excited about it when she got back home that she couldn't wait to tell Donovan. She knew he wouldn't take to the idea right away but she was sure she could persuade him. How many times had he convinced her that something was the right thing to do? But there was no moving him. He wouldn't budge.

"Do what you gotta do, baby girl," is what Eden's father had said, though he gave her absolutely no indication of how to do that. And her mom said what she always said, "no decision is still a decision." Eden's mother always encouraged her to seek out new opportunities and adventures, but seldom offered advice on how to follow through. Eden knew that people in the happiest of marriages weren't happy all the time, and it wasn't even that she wasn't happy. It was that her parents invariably seemed to be on the same page about most things and that wasn't always the case with her and Donovan.

"Don't worry, mom," Celeste said, "we'll help you guys figure this thing out. Celeste picked up her iPad, propped it open on the kitchen island and the familiar ring of the FaceTime app began. After three rings, a young man in his twenties appeared on screen.

"Bryce, bro, we need you on this one," Celeste said to her 26-year-old brother. Bryce, a logistics specialist stationed at Naval Base San Diego, was in the final year of his minimum eight-year service obligation to the U.S. Navy and fortunately wasn't on one of his 24-hour duty shifts.

"Hey baby sis. And what's up, blog chick!" Bryce said to his sisters. Allison started The Blog Chick when she found out she was pregnant with the twins. As thrilled as she was to become a mom, she knew that motherhood would be a rewarding, but often draining experience and she wanted a creative outlet that she could escape to even but for a few minutes. She started blogging about anything that interested her and the blog grew, eventually spawning a podcast of the same name.

"I can't believe you girls. I was going to tell your brother," Eden said, as she listened to Allison and Celeste explain the situation to Bryce.

"So Bry, what do you think?" Allison asked.

"I think this is between mom and dad and we should trust that they will work this out," Bryce said without hesitation. It was at that moment that Donovan walked into the apartment.

"Bryce. This is not the time to be Switzerland. You can't stay neutral about this," Celeste said.

"About what?" Donovan interjected. He walked into the kitchen carrying a sweet-scented string-tied pastry box, the dainty pink package paling in comparison to his imposing figure. He was thickset, 5'11, around 240 pounds, and his neatly-bearded, curvy face sported a broad smile. It was no wonder Eden called him her "teddy bear," and in return, Donovan had nicknamed her "sweetness" because of her penchant for sugary treats.

"Hey, Brycey Bryce! How's everything, son?" Donovan said after seeing his only son on the screen.

"Good, good, good. Been improving my chess game—can't wait to show you how much."

"Oh! Did I just hear a challenge? It's on. I'll be waitin' on ya," Donovan said. Playing chess was one of his favorite things to do and he had taught all of his kids how to play. But only Bryce and

Celeste took to it and neither one of them lived nearby anymore. Donovan kept his skills sharp by playing at the community center every couple of weeks so he looked forward to when he could play with his son again.

"I gotta get going, you guys. Love you, family," Bryce said.

"Love you too," they said in unison as the FaceTime call disconnected.

After eating their quinoa salad and indulging in some sweets, Donovan and Eden headed to their bedroom. The spacious room was sleek and serene with a king-sized platform bed at its center. Hanging directly over the bed was a large custom-framed piece of wall art that featured a heart drawn in the sand on a tropical beach, with Eden and Donovan's names written inside of it--a beautiful reminder of how they had met. Their bedroom was their marital sanctuary but being here tonight was more bittersweet than retreat. Donovan walked into the adjoining bathroom, and Eden sat at her vanity table to remove the little bit of make-up she had on that day. Subtle red highlights layered throughout her chin length bob gave her dark brown hair a hint of color. She loved that she looked several years younger than the fifty-four birthdays she had celebrated.

"You're hella beautiful," Donovan said, walking over to her, his breath minty fresh from having just brushed his teeth.

Eden didn't respond. She got up, slipped out of her dress, and sat on the bed in her matching bra and panties. She worked to keep her body in shape by doing yoga for flexibility, jump roping for cardio, and swimming every now and then at the indoor community pool.

"I hate when we argue, sweetness," Donovan said, taking a seat next to her on the bed.

"Me too," she said, softening just a little, "but I'm not changing my mind about this. This isn't something we can agree to disagree about."

Donovan was ten years older than Eden and though he had traveled to a few places in his life, he was always most comfortable at home. Most of his family were on the east coast and he preferred staying close to them. He liked where he lived and he had planned to retire there. He was looking forward to increasing the amount of time he could spend mentoring local youths at the community center once he no longer had a full-time job. He even thought that perhaps he could become a life coach.

"Eden, you know I want to get into this life coaching thing. I plan to get certified and everything. It wouldn't be full time though so we can enjoy ourselves too," Donovan justified.

"There is such a thing as being a life coach remotely. And the Atlanta youth community need mentors too, you know," Eden said.

"I know, but I want to give back to this community. It just wouldn't be the same, remotely. I want to do hands-on workshops, trips, and confidence-building exercises. All of that works better in person. I want to be here. This is familiar. This is home."

"You know you did this before. I'm not letting you stand in my way this time," Eden said resolutely. Donovan proposed to her eight months after they met, on a snowy New Year's Eve in 1995. A month after that, Eden was accepted into a one-year teaching fellowship program in Boston. Donovan was initially excited for her but then gradually started bringing up reasons why it might not be the best idea.

"We just got engaged. Do you really want to be apart for a whole year?" Donovan asked her.

"It's just a few hours' drive from New York. And it would mean a lot for me to be mentored and gain some hands-on teaching experience. I mean, I won't be able to come back every weekend, but we can make this work, Donovan. Don't you think?" Eden's spirit was dampened, her excitement deflated with every passing minute of their conversation. She ultimately turned down the fellowship and married Donovan in May 1996.

That was twenty-nine years ago and the situation was different this time, but the sentiment was exactly the same. There was an opportunity in front of her that set her soul on fire and she was not about to let Donovan extinguish it. Eden knew how passionate Donovan was about his retirement plan, but she was just as passionate about her new opportunity. Whenever they traveled, she often preferred to stay at a local bed and breakfast instead of a large characterless hotel. Her pie-in-the-sky dream was to run a B&B, meet interesting people and provide a fun, fulfilling getaway for them. When she visited Glitter Cottage, she fell in love with the city and people of Atlanta, and her dream never felt more real.

"You know the youth center wants me to be available for more mentoring after I retire. It's an actual on-the-books position. It's just part-time, but they need me. I've been working with some of those kids since they were young. You didn't start talking seriously about the B&B until you went down there and saw it," Donovan said.

"That's because I thought it wasn't attainable, it was just a dream. But now it looks like everything has lined up and all the signs point to this being my next move," Eden explained.

"All I'm saying is that we settled this already and you agreed to the retirement plan, which meant staying here," Donovan said, realizing that Eden had already tuned him out. The rest of the night was quiet between them. As they laid down together, each hugged their edge of the bed, leaving heavy invisible space between them.

By midnight Celeste had retreated to one of the bedrooms and was fast asleep while Allison sat in the living room working on the next episode of her podcast. Her dad's footsteps startled her as he headed toward the kitchen to sneak a cookie, but he diverted to the living room when he saw the lights were still on.

"What're you doing, hun?" he asked.

"It's a draft of my next blog and podcast topic," she said showing him a couple of hand-written pages.

"Interesting," he said, after reading just a paragraph or two.

"You never listen to my podcasts."

"I know. I just can't sit still and listen to people talking. Probably because I'm used to being the one who's talking," he said, chuckling.

"That's okay, I still love you," Allison said, stretching and yawning her way toward the bedroom. "Promise me you and mom are gonna work this thing out."

"I wish I knew how," he said mostly to himself as Allison had already gone out of earshot.

Eden woke up early and spent most of Saturday with her indefatigable daughters getting everything set up at the community center for the event the following day. She and Donovan spoke only when it was necessary to make sure that nothing fell through the cracks while organizing the event. During a short break for lunch, she took the opportunity to jump on a three-way call with her Atlanta besties.

"Donovan is a good dude, Eden. I don't think you should take it personally that he doesn't want to move," Luciana said.

"No doubt he loves you, Eden, but Luci, how is she not supposed to take it personally?" Sara said.

"I've been going back and forth saying and thinking exactly what you both just said and I just don't know what to do. Maybe a trial separation would give us the space we need to figure some things out?" Eden said to herself more than to them.

"So you're okay with packing up and moving here to run the B&B by calling it a trial separation?" Sara asked.

"I don't know. I prayed on it and I'm trying to keep the faith, but I don't see any solutions right now. I'll talk to you guys later. Thanks so much for listening. Love you." Eden said, ending the call with no more clarity than she had before. It looked like her dream of running the Glitter Cottage bed and breakfast would be bittersweet if it threatened her marriage to a man she truly loved.

The weather was much more August-like by the time Sunday rolled around with temperatures in the low 90s so it felt good to be inside the air-conditioned community center. Ambretta Lane's 40,000 square foot facility housed a full-sized basketball court, running track, swimming pool, and multi-purpose rooms of various sizes. Eden, Donovan, Celeste and Allison walked in sporting their bright orange "Back-To-School" t-shirts, ready to work. During the three-hour event Allison had her digital camera in hand as she was in charge of photographing the day. Eden and Celeste manned the backpack and school supplies giveaway station. And Donovan handed out name tags, greeted everyone, and socialized in his genuinely charming way.

The back-to-school event was designed to not only provide

needed supplies, but to also capture the excitement of the new school year. Eden loved the energy of events like this where she was able to connect with diverse people and learn their stories. It was one of the reasons she enjoyed teaching. It was how she knew that she would love running a bed and breakfast. As she was taking it all in, she saw a friend of Donovan's, Roger Carter, walking over to her. He and Donovan often volunteered together at the community center.

"Eden, what's good?" he said, kissing her lightly on the cheek.

"Can't complain. How've you been?" Eden said.

"I definitely could complain, but who's gonna care, right?" he said, chortling. "Where's your lesser half?"

"Over there somewhere doing what he does best," she said, though not exactly sure where Donovan was.

"He told me that you both are retiring together. That's pretty special. I gotta give it to Donovan though. Still wanting to work so many hours as a mentor when he can just sit back and chill," Roger said.

"Yeah, he said that you guys were pretty persuasive," Eden said.

"Oh yeah, I can twist an arm when I need to. But this was all Donovan. He's the one who approached me about it. Like I said, if it was me retiring, I'd be fishing at a lake near a remote cabin in the woods."

"When did he ask you?" Eden said.

"Last month. I remember because I was about to go on vacation and told him we'd hook up when I was back."

Eden was livid because the timing would have been right after she had gotten back from Atlanta and told Donovan about the

B&B opportunity. He intentionally tried to create a reason for him to stay in Ambretta, Eden thought. She was on her way to confront him when she spotted someone heading her way.

"Hey hey, Eden. Looking good!" said Maxine Davis.

"Hey, Maxie. Haven't seen you in a minute, but I saw your brother at church the other night. I heard he's campaigning to be the next condo board president," Eden said.

"Yeah, Mel is campaigning. It's all he's been talking about lately. What about Donovan? Is he driving you crazy with all this board president stuff?"

"What do you mean?" Eden asked, her eyes widening.

"Oh, did I get it wrong? Mel said Donovan was at the campaign meeting Friday afternoon. I assumed that meant he was running too."

"Oh, I'm sure it's some kind of mix up. You know, I see my daughters over there looking for me. Good seeing you, Maxie," Eden said, scurrying to get away from the place where her husband's betrayal had just been revealed. She filled Celeste and Allison in on what happened and they were slack-jawed to learn that their father could be this deceitful. Having no real advice to give their mother, they simply offered their love and support.

"I'm heading back to Philly now, mom, but please call me later and let me know what's going on with you and dad," Celeste felt powerless, but hopeful.

"Mom, do you want to come home with me for a little while?" Allison offered.

"No, dad and I need to hash this out. Right now," Eden said, as she hugged and said goodbye to the compassionate daughters she raised.

By all accounts, the back-to-school event was a success and Eden was grateful that the clean-up crew was there to wrap things up so that she and Donovan could head out. The summer sun was just starting to set by the time they arrived home, an orange glow illuminating through the living room windows. They sat across from each other with Donovan in his favorite armchair and Eden on the matching loveseat.

"So you just flat out lied to me? You said that the youth center reached out to you. That was a lie. And you sure as hell didn't tell me that you were running for board president. That was a whopper of a lie by omission. What's your excuse this time?" Eden asked.

"I have some fresh ideas to bring to this development and being board president can help me implement them," he explained to Eden, "I have everything I need here: family, friends, love, work. It's familiar. My favorite barber, the gym, the way Mabo Lake freezes over at Christmas, playing chess at the community center, the local Thanksgiving parade. I don't mind traveling, but this is what I want to come home to.

"I don't want to be stuck here for the next three or four years until you're done doing all the things you want to do. I'm not missing another opportunity because of you," Eden said before storming off into another room.

Since his wife was boiling mad and since his daughters had gone home, Donovan decided to sleep in one of the other bedrooms that night. Meanwhile, Eden was in bed trying to calm herself. Before going to sleep, she prayed as she always did. Waking up with the morning light of a new day to inspire her, Eden had come to a decision. She was confident in the resolution because she had made it from a position of going towards something she wanted, not running away from something she didn't want.

"Donovan. I love you. I love us. But I also need to love me. I think we need some time away from each other. So at the end of the school year, I'll be moving to Atlanta. We can call it a trial separation," she said to a stunned Donovan that Monday morning.

"You know that's not what I want. That's ten months from now. A lot can happen between now and then," Donovan said.

"Really, like what?" she asked.

Donovan didn't have a response. He was afraid to tell his wife that he was terrified to step out of his comfort zone. For the next several days Donovan dug down in his soul, seeking out a way to not let his deep-seated fear of change destroy the intense bond he had with his wife. His love for her was mind-blowing yet he was at a loss on how to fix things. His wife believed in looking for signs from God, from the Universe, about when and how to proceed. He decided that the very least he could do was to be open to that for himself.

Two weeks later was the first day of school in the Ambretta community, so Donovan knew that Eden wouldn't be home until after 4pm. He sat in his car thinking about everything that had led up to that moment and he knew he was wrong. He finally said out loud to himself what he had always known.

"I can't grow inside of a comfort zone because it's designed to keep me comfortable. I can only grow if and when I decide to step out of it."

It was what he must have said to his daughters somewhere along the way because they had grown into courageous and capable young women. He was proud of them and it inspired him.

Donovan turned the dial on his dashboard to pull up Allison's podcast and began listening.

Allison:

"Hey everyone, this is Allison, your favorite blog chick. I've been thinking a lot about relationships this week and growing apart. Sibling to sibling, mother to daughter, father to son, husband to wife, friend to friend. Dr. Lorraine Hudson is here today to talk to us exactly about that…growing apart and how to identify the signs."

Although Donovan had read a little of the draft that Allison had shown him, it hit differently hearing her speak from the heart to her listening audience. Today, he was one of those listeners so he continued to do so as he sat in his parked car on Main Street.

Dr. Hudson:

"I find that couples often have conflict the most over things like finances, sex, and housework, but something that's just as important in a relationship, in any relationship, is finding ways to stay connected. Sometimes there are underlying reasons why people aren't connected in a relationship, like the age difference dynamic, or a lack of shared goals. It may create a power imbalance where the younger person may feel like they're giving something up to be in the relationship with the older person."

Hearing those words made something click for Donovan. It was the sign he was looking for and it had opened him up from the inside, allowing insight to pour in. He realized that because of his age and sense of responsibility, he had played the role of a father figure for Eden. He hadn't treated her as an equal in some ways. And it was never something he intended. He wasn't her mentor. He was her husband and he loved her. He had figured that as long as he was taking care of things for his wife and family, then everybody won. He had mistakenly believed that his happiness was automatically Eden's happiness. Donovan sat silent as he listened to the rest of the podcast, allowing the enlightenment from it wash over him.

Allison:

"Thank you for being with us today, Dr. Hudson. And thank you, my Chick listeners for spending some time with me today. As always, signing off for now with gratitude and a challenge to everyone who can hear my voice, to make today one that you won't forget."

The first day of school was a welcome distraction for Eden. When she had told Sara and Luciana about the trial separation, they had mixed emotions about the situation because they liked Donovan. Eden loved Donovan, but she had no regrets about her decision. She arrived home at half past four to find the signature pastry box from Viv & Vera's sitting on the kitchen island.

"Snickerdoodles not gonna do it this time, buddy," she said

out loud to herself, and then she read the handwritten note that was resting on top of the box:

Sweetness, please give me one more chance to show you how much I love you and to tell you how sorry I am. I'm in the neighborhood but want to give you some time to yourself. Call me when it's okay to come home. Please open the box…just one more time. Love, your teddy bear.

"Fat chance," Eden said as she left the box unopened and then worked on some lesson plans for the classes she was teaching this year. Forty-five minutes had passed by the time Eden checked her silenced phone to see that she had a voicemail from Celeste and texts from Allison and Bryce. They all said the same thing: *Mom, open the box.*

When she finally opened it, there were no snickerdoodles or pastries of any kind inside. There were only random pieces of paper that looked as though they had been printed from various websites. One was from Joe's Barbershop. One was from Buff Gym. One was from Be A Life Coach certification class. One was from City Chess Club. And the one thing they had in common was that they were all located in Atlanta. There was a note at the bottom of the box that read: "You are my familiar. You are my home."

Eden sat in silence, allowing the magnitude of the moment to wash over her, and then she texted her husband and kids to let them know that she had opened the box. Donovan arrived home twenty minutes later carrying another pastry box that he placed on the glass coffee table in the living room where Eden was waiting for him. He folded her into his embrace and she melted into the warmth of his tender heart. They lingered in the hug for a moment, releasing only to bring their lips together in familiar intimacy before sitting down side by side on the loveseat.

"Eden, you are more important than any place I would ever want to live," Donovan said. "I was afraid. That's why I always stuck close to home and close to family. That's why I planned everything so that I could always make the safe choice. I am so sorry."

"I love you so much for saying that. But I own up to my part in what got us here too, Donovan. I hate to say it, but I willingly turned over control of my happiness to another person. It's an inside job and always has been. I realize that now. I thought I had lost connection with you, but really I lost connection with myself," Eden said.

"You are smart, spiritual, and hella sexy. You are the center of my world, Eden. But you are also your own world and I want to be there to support you in it. Whenever and wherever," Donovan said, letting her know that he had already dropped out of the condo board president race and that he was actually looking forward to living in a warmer climate. And since they couldn't afford to own two homes, Donovan had arranged for their son-in-law, Jace, to sublet their Ambretta apartment. Allison would use it as her podcast studio and her parents would have a place to stay when they came to visit.

"Just promise me that we can come back every year to see Mabo Lake frozen over at Christmas," Donovan said, hugging her tight to his chest. "I love you."

"I love you too, Donovan," Eden said, feeling awakened, aligned, and in awe of her blessings. She slowly pulled away from her teddy bear of a husband and slid the pink pastry box toward her. When she opened this one, it was filled to the brim with her favorite sugary treat. She smiled, took a bite of the snickerdoodle, and savored the sweetness of it all.

'TIS THE SEASON

I t was a typical snowy December morning in the New York City suburb of Westchester county. The Ambretta Lane condominium complex was beautifully bathed in winter white landscape, nearby Mabo Lake was frozen over, and the slick icy walking trail surrounding it was anything but walkable. Local stores were having Christmas, Kwanzaa, Hannukah, and New Year's Eve holiday sales almost simultaneously while faux-bearded Salvation Army Santas rang bells on a couple of street corners with familiar festive tunes playing in the background. Decorative signs in store windows served as reminders of Ambretta's anniversary celebration. The event that had taken more than a year to plan was just a week away. The whole community was abuzz about what the evening would bring and many were concerned that there would not be much to celebrate going into the new year. A board meeting was taking place three days before the anniversary celebration and there were rumors of an investor takeover of the current board which meant that condo owners were at risk of possibly losing their residences. There had been an influx of new residents who had no prior connection to the community and unfortunately wanted to change a lot of what made it special.

Though Maxine was a little nervous about what the outcome might be, her mind was elsewhere as she sat in her double-parked black Honda Civic oblivious to the flurry of Saturday morning activities happening on the avenue. She had a little more holiday shopping to do and still needed to decorate the Christmas tree that stood bare in her living room. Fortunately, she was off from work for the remainder of the year so she was happy about having the time to get everything done. She had already thanked her boss for her spa day Christmas gift and had replied to the holiday greetings from some of her co-workers but Maxine remembered that she had forgotten one. She took her phone out of her leather tote bag and started typing to send a text.

Hey Heather, just wanted to thank you for the secret Santa gift. It's a beautiful journal. Can't wait to use it and hope you're having fun! Happy Holidays!

Heather Weiss was a 26-year-old administrative assistant who had just started working at the job right before Thanksgiving. Maxine didn't know much about her except that she was very friendly and likeable. Heather was excited about going skiing for the holidays so she missed the department celebration but had made sure to leave a gift for her secret Santa. Maxine really did think it was a beautiful journal, a small black book with the words "Trust. Believe. Act." spelled out in gold letters, but she wasn't big on writing down her thoughts so Maxine was pretty sure she wouldn't be using it.

She checked the time and realized that she had been waiting awhile for Brandon to come out of *Anna's Gems and Things* where he went to buy a Christmas gift for his girlfriend. It tickled her to see her one and only child smack dab in the middle of puppy love. Brandon had met Amber when they were in high school band together and what started as a friendship eventually grew into a budding romance over the past year. They were both seniors, graduating in June, and heading to college after that. Brandon's plan was to apply to only tri-state area colleges in New York, New Jersey and Connecticut in the hopes that he and Amber would be continuing their relationship after high school. Brandon was very different from his father in most ways, but in the romance department, he and Nate were just alike. They both gave their whole hearts to the women they loved.

Nate Montgomery. Maxine had been thinking a lot about him lately though not by choice. Every time he called to chat with Brandon, Nate always seemed to maneuver Maxine into the conversation and into reminiscing about the good old days when they first met. It was the third day of tenth grade and the two 15-year-olds happened to be seated next to each other in the last row of their English 101 classroom. Maxine was always self-conscious in school because she was almost thirty pounds heavier than most other girls in her class. Nate was athletic, popular, and had a slew of teen girls vying for his attention, especially sexy Soraya. It was literally how classmates referred to the slender, attractive 16-year-old who always wore tight cloth-ing and Chanel as her signature scent. Soraya made the most of every opportunity she had to talk to Nate. They shared a love of baseball and both hoped to become lawyers. But it was Maxine who ended up becoming best friends with Nate, bonding over their love of oldies music and the loss of both of their moms. Their friendship eventually led to dating and then marriage. Nate and Maxine tied the knot at city hall two months after high school graduation, moved into a small New York City apartment that Nate's lawyer father gifted them after Nate promised that he would study Pre-Law at NYU and continue on to law school. Being married and living together was exciting, romantic and short-lived. It didn't take long for things to fall apart when Maxine's jealousy and insecurities clashed with Nate's long hours of attending and studying in college. They had been married for just under a year, but it was long enough for Maxine to realize that they were too young and naïve to make a marriage work. Nate reluctantly agreed to a divorce and years later moved to Miami when the law firm he was working for relocated. Brandon was 7. Maxine was 27 and heartbroken.

Maxine's phone vibrated in her hand, alerting her to a text message.

Maxie, did you call him yet? It was the third text from her 39-year-old brother in the past hour. Melvin was being a royal pain in the ass as usual and she was mad at herself for thinking their sibling relationship would be different once they had become adults. Maxine was three years younger than Melvin and she loved him but sometimes she didn't like him very much. Saying no to him meant that he was going to ask her ten more times to make sure that she was committed to that initial no. And for the past few months, since he had become the new condo board president, he had been stressing the hell out of her about Ambretta's legal issues.

"Yeah man, I called him. Alright? You know, you could've called him yourself," Maxine said into the phone, deciding to call her annoying brother instead of enduring the volley of text messages.

"I did but he's taking more than a minute getting back to me. So can he help the board out? I mean, he is still licensed in New York, right?" Melvin's baritone voice raised an octave when he was impatient.

"Yes and yes. He said he'll call you tonight."

"Way to come through, Nate! I always liked that dude. Big time real estate lawyer. My one-time brother-in-law. Maybe you should think about starting things up with him again. Or is he off the market? Because I'm thinking, he's a pretty good catch, and I mean, he is Brandon's father," Melvin said.

"Bye, Mel," Maxine said, desperate to get off this topic.

"Bye, sis. Love you."

"Yeah, yeah," Maxine said, before ending the call. She knew that her brother was right about one thing. Nate was a good catch. He was a well-respected attorney in the real estate world, average in looks, but sexy as hell. And according to Brandon, Nate wasn't seriously dating anyone. Not that it mattered to Maxine. No, it didn't matter that she still remembered every muscle of his smooth bronze physique. And it didn't matter that they were each other's first lovers. Her very platonic relationship with her ex had blossomed into a genuine friendship over the past couple of years.

Maxine often felt overwhelmed having juggled three separate

relationships with three very different men. Mother to Brandon, her growing young man; sister to Melvin, her emotionally needy brother; and ex-wife to Nate, her first true love and father of her only child. It was too much to think about. She needed a mindless distraction, so she clicked on the Blog Chick podcast right after Brandon had texted to say that he still couldn't decide what to buy Amber that was within his $40 budget.

Allison:

"Hey everyone, this is Allison, your favorite blog chick. This is my final podcast of the year so let's make it a good one. I don't know about you, but for me, this is my favorite time of year. It's the time of year that I take stock, look back, look at what's right in front of me and be grateful. Let's get ready to release and end those things, situations, and people that no longer align with who we want to be. Let's clear that space and see what wonderfulness fills it. 'Tis the season to expect the unexpected."

"Easy for her to say," Maxine said out loud to herself, clicking the podcast off and glancing through the window to see Brandon finally emerging from the store, his face sullen. He opened the car door and sank into the passenger seat.

"What happened?" Maxine asked, readying herself to fight and defend her son from whatever injustice had just occurred in the jewelry store.

"I don't want to talk about it, mom."

"Either you talk about it or I march into that store and start asking questions," Maxine said, having already unbuckled her seat belt and unlocked the car door.

"Mom, no. It's nothing like that. It's Amber. She just texted me. She broke up with me."

"Oh, honey. I'm so sorry," Maxine said. She knew what it was like to be hurt and let down by a first love. She remembered all too well. Maxine reached across the seat to hug Brandon but he pulled away.

"Can we just go home, please?"

Maxine was happy to do just that as she drove to their street and pulled into her dedicated parking spot in the garage. She walked into her apartment and quickly traded her winter boots for the comfy slippers waiting near the front door, tossed her coat and bag to the side, and plopped on the couch. She saw that Brandon was heading to his room with his head down low.

"Hey Bran, come sit with your mom for a minute," she said, gesturing him towards the spot next to her on the couch.

"I just want to be by myself for a little while."

"You can absolutely do that, but let's chat for a bit first."

Brandon sat down next to her, his hat and jacket still on. Maxine removed the hat and placed it on the coffee table in front of them. She gently lifted his chin up and could see that he was fighting back tears.

"Sweetheart. I know this hurts."

"I'm alright," he said, his voice cracking.

"Yeah, you will be. Falling in love is no joke and like anything worth having, it sometimes requires that you take a leap of faith. To be honest, that's something I'm just learning to do at my age. Listen, I just want you to know that I'm proud of you for taking a chance on love, putting your heart on the line for someone you cared about."

"But why didn't she love me back?"

"I don't know, Bran. But what I do know is that you're a cool dude, an amazing human being, and there's an awesome young lady out there somewhere who is looking to fall in love with someone just like you. So let us both make the most of the holidays, okay? You know, it is the season to expect the unexpected," she said, blatantly stealing the line from the Blog Chick's podcast today.

Maxine kissed him on the cheek and wrapped her arms around his 6'2" frame. Brandon retreated to his room and Maxine went into the bathroom to wash the stress of the day off her face. She looked in the bathroom mirror and took in her warm brown features. She had her father's defined jawline and deep-set eyes. And she had inherited her mother's oval face, thin straight hair, and low self-esteem, which was why she was never really satisfied with what she saw in the mirror. Even after shedding 45 pounds two years after giving birth to Brandon, Maxine's confidence about her physical appearance was fleeting. Her mom, Portia, hadn't raised her to have much self-confidence because she herself had low self-esteem. Portia wasn't bad looking but most people would not call her attractive. She believed and taught Maxine that only pretty girls got what they wanted in this world including the best men. Portia's choices in male partners reflected what she thought she deserved and she ended up with guys who treated her the way she expected. It was pure luck that she met and married Maxine's dad, Melvin Sr., who was a decent guy but true to form, Portia's self-loathing destroyed the relationship six years into it. She had already given birth to Maxine and Melvin Jr. but wasn't emotionally available to them for most of their childhood. It seemed that most of Maxine's male relationships had been dysfunctional too, but she was determined to do better than her mom had. Portia passed away shortly before Maxine turned 14 and her dad died four years later, right before her high school graduation. Maxine was an orphan and devastated. She felt that she needed professional help to fully process the death of her parents and deal with the baggage of insecurities she brought into her romantic relationships. She tried therapy once but it wasn't a positive experience and was one in which she felt judged, so she never went back. Instead, she dabbled in self-help books and podcasts from time to time to keep herself afloat and once even attended a virtual weekend women's conference. To her surprise, it had all helped her to identify and start processing some of the feelings of insecurity that she had been living with.

Most of Maxine's romantic relationships after Nate were seasonal, not lasting more than three months. She had always found a reason to get out or mess it up before her partner beat her to it. But her most recent relationship, two years of seriously dating Perry Armstrong, was pretty normal and healthy. Maxine liked his sense of humor, his funky fashion style, and his willingness to try anything once. Unfortunately, she found out during a fun night of truth or dare that Perry once had a relationship with a guy. And though he said it was a one-time thing and that he was strictly into women, that was a bridge too far for Maxine's insecurities to cross. That was three years ago and since then she hadn't dated much, instead choosing to focus on being a good mom to Brandon and holding it down at work. She hadn't gone to college but she was able to land a job as a data entry clerk at a gaming company and eventually rose to the level of junior data analyst.

Maxine enjoyed her job but she also looked forward to the end-of-the-year break and some much-needed down time. She had gotten a text from Nate letting her know that he connected with her brother and that they had already strategized a plan that would hopefully protect the condo board. By 6:30 that evening, Brandon had decided to go to the movies with a couple of his friends, and Maxine had already begun decompressing from the stresses of the day. She had taken a shower and was stretched out on the couch with a cup of hot chocolate, a Christmas sugar cookie, and a crossword puzzle at her side, with an oldies R&B playlist playing in the background. She nestled into the cushion of the couch and into the comfort of the evening. The unexpected chime of the lobby doorbell startled her and when she checked the security camera from her phone, she was shocked to see Nate standing there. Nate, who she had just texted with hours before, who was supposed to be in Miami. Maxine buzzed him in, turned down the music, and opened the apartment door as he approached from the elevator.

"Hey. What're you doing here?"

"Are you gonna let me in," Nate asked, with a wicked smile and a soft chuckle.

She gestured for him to come in and he took a seat in the overstuffed chair next to the couch.

"You hungry? Want something to drink?" Maxine said.

"Nah, I'm good," Nate said, smiling as his eyes traveled the length of Maxine's body. She was wearing silk pajama bottoms with a matching silk top.

"So why are you in town?" Maxine asked, sitting back down on the couch with her legs crossed.

"A few reasons. I thought it made sense to be here in person for Wednesday's board meeting. I also wanted to check on Brandon." Nate paused. "And I wanted to see you. "You're looking good, Maxie."

"Well, thank you."

"Hey, do you ever think about me?"

"You're Brandon's father, so of course I think about you. You're a good role model for him."

"You know that's not what I mean. Do you ever think about me? Me and you?"

"Nate, you hurt me," were the words Maxine hadn't planned to say but somehow they were sitting on the tip of her tongue. Their short-lived marriage had been eleven months of mistrust and jealousy, mostly on her part, that ended in infidelity and divorce. Maxine's memory of the night that ruined their marriage was still vivid.

"How the hell are you just getting home?" Maxine had said, "It's almost 2:15 in the morning."

Nate was usually done with his college classes, studying, and any extracurricular activities by 10pm and home by 10:30pm. Maxine was usually still up but on this night, she had a tension headache from a hectic day at work. She was the administrative assistant in charge of planning a sales conference at the gaming company she worked for and it was stressful. She took some Tylenol, dimmed the lights in the apartment and fell asleep on the couch around 9pm. When she woke up four hours later, she quickly checked the kitchen, bathroom and bedroom to see that

Nate wasn't home yet. So when he came tipping in after 2am, all of her suspicions and jealousy took center stage.

"I'm asking you again. Where the hell have you been?"

"A bunch of us from pre-law met at Ricky's Bar to celebrate someone's birthday. I'm a little late and a little tipsy, okay? I just want to take a shower and go to bed," Nate said. He took off his jacket and walked toward the bathroom.

"Whose birthday was it?" Maxine stepped in front of him.

"Let's not do this. I'm tired," Nate said.

"Whose birthday was it?" she repeated.

"It was Soraya's okay. It's not a big deal."

"Soraya? Who the hell is Soraya?" Maxine's eyes widened. "Wait a fucking minute. Are you talking about Soraya from high school—Sexy Soraya? What's she got to do with your pre-law friends?"

"She studying pre-law at NYU too, Maxie. We're in a couple of the same classes. I didn't tell you because I know how you can get. It's not a big deal."

"Did you sleep with her tonight?" Maxine asked, remembering how Soraya always had a thing for Nate and would probably do anything to be with him.

"No, I didn't. Okay, are we done with this now?" Nate said.

"Yeah, okay. Just one more question. Have you slept with her since we've been married."

Nate was silent and frozen in place.

"Please don't make me ask you again, Nate."

"I...I don't want to do this, Maxie. Let's both go to sleep and talk tomorrow."

"I knew it. I always knew you would cheat on me. And with

Soraya of all people. Guess I'm not skinny or sexy enough for you. I've always been just the true-blue friend but apparently not good enough to be your wife. Got it."

Twenty-year-old Maxine left Nate in early June and by August she knew she was pregnant. She had moved back home to Ambretta Lane to live with her brother, Melvin. Their parents' combined life insurance had provided them with just enough money to maintain the condo apartment. Maxine had already filed for divorce, but she decided to keep the baby and not tell Nate about it. It would have kept her tied to him and that was the last thing she wanted because she didn't think she could trust him as a husband or a father.

Guilt had gotten the best of her though because baby Brandon looked exactly like Nate every time he smiled, so Maxine eventually came clean to Nate that he had a son. He was livid that she waited so long to tell him and lashed out in anger saying that he wanted nothing to do with her or the baby. But a few weeks later, he showed up at Maxine's doorstep with gifts for his son, who was seven months old and already crawling. Even though Nate had spent just one unplanned night with Soraya, it was enough for Maxine to believe that she was following in her mom's footsteps that always seemed to lead to the wrong guy. But Nate wasn't the wrong guy and the two of them had come a long way since the end of their marriage. Though they never rekindled their romantic relationship, Nate and Maxine figured out how to co-parent, tackling situations as they arose. The mature man sitting next to her was decent and still apologetic after all these years.

"I know. It was one time. I was 22, immature, cocky, and stupid. And I am so sorry that I hurt you." Nate allowed his grown-man apology to settle for a couple of seconds. "But Maxie, you hurt me too…when you waited until my son was 6 months old to tell me about him."

"I know. But I never would have done what I did if you hadn't cheated on me.…you know what? I really don't want to talk about this. That was 17 years ago. The past is past. We're good. We managed to raise an incredible son and I'm grateful that Brandon has you in his life."

"It really messed me up when you didn't tell me about Brandon. I was in love with you, Maxie. I'm still…in love with you."

Maxine was immediately triggered because she knew that she still loved him too. But deep down inside there was a part of her that was an insecure 20-year-old who was afraid of being hurt, despite her insistence that "the past is past."

"Let's not do this, Nate. You and I are in a good place. We're good friends and we're good parents," she said, rising from the couch. She walked over to the door and unlocked it. "I'll tell Brandon to call you when he gets home or better yet, you can text him yourself."

"Yeah, I'll do that." Nate took a couple of steps toward the door and then stopped short and turned when he heard a familiar song playing in the background. "Maxie, turn that up. That's our song," Nate said, picking up her phone and tapping the volume button on the side.

"No, you're leaving," Maxine said, grabbing the phone from him and physically directing him back toward the door.

"Stop playing," he said. "This was our joint back in the day." Their love of R&B duo Ashford & Simpson was something they had in common.

"C'mon, boo. You know how we do," Nate said, grooving to the soulful rhythm of *Is It Still Good To Ya*. He took Maxine's hand, gently twirled her around once and began belting out the words to the song. Maxine's steely resolve slowly melted into sweet teen memories of days long gone, and for a moment she was swept up as she joined him in singing to their song. But as that oldie transitioned to the next song the two of them were still holding on to each other from their impromptu dance.

"Maxie, marry me," Nate said, holding her a little tighter.

That momentous Saturday night seemed to meld into the next Saturday because Maxine could not recall how she had made it through the week. The all-important board meeting had come and gone and tonight was Ambretta's 25th anniversary of the condominium complex. When she walked into the beautifully bedecked community center, Maxine was impressed to see her big brother's leadership and hard work come to fruition. His over-bearing personality aside, Melvin had pulled everything together with the help of a lot of dedicated volunteers from the Ambretta community. There were twelve white linen-covered round tables with eight banquet chairs and a winter white and green floral centerpiece on each table. A festively decorated 6-foot-long stage was front and center in the room with the neighborhood's self-proclaimed DJ extraordinaire, Reggie, checking his equipment. There was a large projector screen above the stage displaying audio and video of the Ambretta community highlights over the past 25 years and many of its residents, past and present, where there in the room for the celebration.

Maxine sat at her pre-assigned table and looked around the room in search of her son. Brandon had been in a much better mood the past couple of days and he seemed a little too excited to come to the event with her, having left before her to meet up with his friends. She hadn't spotted him yet but she did see other familiar faces like the flirty but harmless head of Ambretta security, Gerald, who was sitting with his heavy-set, beautifully-dressed wife. Previous condo board president, Claudi Pruitt, was cozied up near the bar in an intimate conversation with an attractive woman who looked to be in her early 60s. Viv and Vera, owners of the local tea shop, beamed with pride over the decadent dessert display they had contributed to the event. And the Blog Chick herself, Allison Waymond, who was sitting at a table with her husband, was intensely focused on her iPad, likely capturing the spirit of the evening for her next podcast.

Being in the midst of so many people who represented the history of Ambretta, Maxine allowed her nostalgic surroundings to transport her back to when she and Nate were just teens hanging out at all the cool places in the community. Sitting in the grass at Mabo Lake Park was where she first told Nate about her feelings of inadequacies stemming from the relationship with her mom. Sharing cheese fries and milkshakes at the local diner was where they also shared their goals and dreams. In a parked car in the lot behind the closed library was where they had sex for the first time. Maxine realized that her doubts had nothing to do with Nate. She knew that he genuinely loved her, but she spent most of her adult life not knowing why. She was certain that he could have had his pick of women who were more attractive and sophisticated than she was. A woman perhaps who was a lawyer like Nate would have been a better partner for him. Maxine was smart but she had not gone to college. She had spent too much time doubting herself, wondering if she was worthy of someone loving her for who she was. But she had made progress in her self-perception and the doubts had started to dissolve. It had been a week since Nate proposed and Maxine had replayed last Saturday night's conversation over and over in her mind.

"Maxie, marry me," Nate had said.

"You play too much," Maxine said, taking a step back from him.

"Do I sound like I'm playing? I'm straight up serious," he said.

"But…we're friends."

"We've always been more than friends. We've known each other almost our whole lives. Our love created Brandon. And my love for you is the same as it ever was. Do you love me, Maxie?"

"I do, Nate. But marriage is a commitment and I'm not sure I can do it."

"We've always had the connection and now we have the maturity to make it work. So is it that you don't want to or that you're afraid to?"

Maxine knew it was fear. During her two-year relationship with Perry, she started thinking about what she would say if Perry had asked her to marry him. She felt ready back then, but she couldn't quite get her heart and mind to the finish line to be able to say yes and their subsequent breakup seemed to validate her fear. But this was different. This was Nate. They had been married before. He was her first love and the father of her child. And he was here, wearing his heart on his sleeve. There was no question that she loved him, and she had come a long way in dealing with her trust issues. The bottom line was that she was just scared to take the leap.

"How would it work anyway? You're in Miami and I'm not in a position to leave my job right now to move to another state," Maxine reasoned.

"You wouldn't have to." Nate said. "I'm moving back to New York. It's something I've been planning for a while, but I just got a job offer at a new law firm and it's based right here."

"What happens if I say no?"

"I'm still moving here for work. I'm still Brandon's father. And we'll still be friends."

"Okay, okay, okay. I'm gonna need a minute to take this all in, and by a minute, I mean I'm gonna need some time."

"I'm not sure if I'm going to the anniversary celebration, but I'll be in New York all this week and then flying back to Miami on Sunday morning. I know I kinda sprung this on you, Maxie, so take all the time you need."

"Hey, Brandon doesn't know about this, does he?"

"No. I wouldn't want to get his hopes up if it doesn't happen."

Maxine had turned that conversation over in her heart and mind all week. She wasn't sure if Nate was going to show up to tonight's celebration but she was sure about her answer to his marriage proposal. The certainty of her decision came on the heels of a tragedy. She had gotten a text from a co-worker, followed by a phone call. It was concerning Heather Weiss. She had been in a car accident on an icy road while on vacation and was in serious but stable condition at the hospital. After hearing the news, Maxine picked up the journal that she had received from Heather. Although she didn't know her well, Maxine shed a few tears for the vivacious young woman whose life would be forever impacted by what happened. She instinctively opened the journal and began furiously writing down every emotion and thought that came through her. By the time she was done, she had reached a moment of clarity.

Someone from behind placing their arms around her for a gentle hug brought Maxine back to the present moment. She turned to see her son standing there with a pretty young lady.

"Mom, hi. This is Brianna," Brandon said.

"Hi, nice to meet you," Brianna said, extending her bejeweled hand to shake Maxine's.

"Nice to meet you too, Brianna. Are you guys enjoying the celebration so far?"

"Yeah. We were just at the photo booth—see?" Brianna said, pulling out a strip of photos from her strapless fuchsia pocket dress.

"You guys look great." Maxine couldn't help but notice the permanent smile on her son's face.

"Bran, I'm gonna go catch up with my friends. See you later," Brianna said, bouncing her way through the other party guests. Her bubbly personality was infectious.

"So, she seems nice," Maxine said, as Brandon sat down next to her.

"Yeah, she's pretty cool. I met her last week when I went to the movies with my friends. She's a freshman at Iona and works part-time at the movie concession stand on weekends."

"Well, I'm glad you made a new friend."

"Me too. I didn't actually believe you at first, but it's like you said, this is the season to expect the unexpected."

Maxine was always caught off guard when hearing her words come out of Brandon's mouth. As a mom, she knew that her lessons and advice didn't always get absorbed by the human she gave birth to, so it was often a pleasant surprise when one took root.

"Okay, I'll see you later," Brandon said, standing up to leave. "Oh, there's dad," he said before disappearing into the crowd.

"Hey, beautiful," Nate said, taking a seat next to her.

"Hey, I thought you weren't coming," Maxine said.

"I hadn't really planned to but your brother wanted me to be here and you know how persistent he can be."

They both laughed and the crackle of the microphone directed everyone's attention to the stage where Melvin, as condo board president, was about to give opening remarks.

"I'd like to welcome you all to this well-deserved 25th anniversary celebration of an incredible community of people. I'll start by addressing the elephant in the room which is the status of Ambretta's board of directors. It's my pleasure to share with you that we are on solid footing again and have expertly and successfully handled the situation with the investors. Thank you all for the time and effort you put in to help create this positive outcome. And a special shout out to Nate Montgomery for his valuable contribution as our legal consultant."

Nate nodded in appreciation and there was applause and congratulations all around for everyone involved.

"So we're going to hand out awards to recognize some very deserving Ambretta residents and after that, we'll party hearty!" Melvin said, while doing a quick two-step to the delight of the room.

Thirty minutes later, the buffet was open, liquor was flowing, music was playing and the dance floor was full.

Nate stood up extended his hand toward Maxine. "May I have this dance?"

"I'd be happy to, Mr. Montgomery, but only if you ask me again using my name." Maxine stood up and took his hand.

"May I please have this dance, Maxine Davis."

"I think you mean Maxine Davis-soon-to-be-Maxine-Montgomery, again." She couldn't help but laugh out loud to see the stunned look on Nate's face.

"Stop playing."

"I'm straight up serious."

"I don't want to jinx this by asking, but what made you decide?"

"Let's just say that life can be unpredictable. We always think we have enough time to do everything we want and in an instant that can all change. So I'm ready and can't wait to be your wife again."

"I love you, Maxie."

"I love you too. Always have."

The Ambretta Lane 25th anniversary celebration was a success by all accounts and Melvin basked in the glory of his part in it. Ambretta Lane was a place with interesting people and unique stories spread throughout six modern condominium buildings. The community was ripe with romances and rivalries, triumphs and sorrows, heartbreak and happy endings.

Maxine Davis found her happiness in reuniting with her first love and seeing the expression on Brandon's face when she and Nate told him their news. She wore her new 1.5 carat diamond pear-shaped engagement ring proudly and was excited about her future with Nate. She was hopeful about life in general. Maxine received word that Heather was going to pull through in her recovery from the car accident and she was relieved. Maxine was ready to walk into the new year with a new outlook. She realized that there is a season for everything in life. Her first marriage to Nate wasn't the right time for either of them. This was their unexpected season and it was more than welcome.

About the Author

Valerie Gilford Collins is a creative writer who has won Honorable Mention for her short story, "Memories Get In The Way" in the 2009 National Writers Digest competition. Ambretta Lane is her debut collection of short stories. She has a Bachelor of Arts in English and resides in New York.

Visit ambrettalane.com to learn more about the author and the Ambretta Lane stories.

www.ingramcontent.com/pod-product-compliance
Lightning Source LLC
Chambersburg PA
CBHW061127100726
47911CB00013B/706